LOST IN
THE MOMENT
AND FOUND

LOST IN THE MOMENT AND FOUND

SEANAN McGUIRE

TOR PUBLISHING GROUP

NEW YORK

This is a work of fiction. All of the characters, organizations, and events portrayed in this novel are either products of the author's imagination or are used fictitiously.

LOST IN THE MOMENT AND FOUND

Copyright © 2022 by Seanan McGuire

All rights reserved.

Interior illustrations by Rovina Cai

A Tordotcom Book
Published by Tom Doherty Associates/Tor Publishing Group
120 Broadway
New York, NY 10271

www.tor.com

Tor® is a registered trademark of Macmillan Publishing Group, LLC.

Library of Congress Cataloging-in-Publication Data

Names: McGuire, Seanan, author.
Title: Lost in the moment and found / Seanan McGuire.
Description: First Edition. | New York : Tom Doherty Associates
Book, 2023. | Series: Wayward children ; 8
Identifiers: LCCN 2022028071 (print) | LCCN 2022028072 (ebook) |
ISBN 9781250213631 (hardcover) | ISBN 9781250213648 (ebook)
Subjects: LCGFT: Novels.
Classification: LCC PS3607.R36395 L67 2023 (print) |
LCC PS3607.R36395 (ebook) | DDC 813/.6—dc23/eng/20220624
LC record available at https://lccn.loc.gov/2022028071
LC ebook record available at https://lccn.loc.gov/2022028072

Our books may be purchased in bulk for promotional, educational, or business use. Please contact your local bookseller or the Macmillan Corporate and Premium Sales Department at 1-800-221-7945, extension 5442, or by email at MacmillanSpecialMarkets@macmillan.com.

First Edition: 2023

Printed in the United States of America

0 9 8 7 6 5 4 3 2 1

FOR THE CHILD I WAS.
I WILL SPEND MY ENTIRE LIFE
TRYING TO MAKE UP FOR THE FACT THAT
WHEN I WAS YOU, I DIDN'T RUN SOON ENOUGH.
I'M SORRY.

AUTHOR'S NOTE

While all the Wayward Children books have dealt with heavy themes and childhood traumas, this one addresses an all-too-familiar monster: the one that lives in your own home. Themes of grooming and adult gaslighting are present in the early text. As a survivor of something very similar, I would not want to be surprised by these elements where I didn't expect them.

I just want to offer you this reassurance: Antsy runs. Before anything can actually happen, Antsy runs.

Street penny sacrament; what are you looking for?
Lost in the moment and found,
I am the God of Lost Things, and I will take care of you.
Foundling and fallen, not where it ought to be,
Mislaid and moved around.
I am the God of Lost Things, and I will take care of you.

I will take care of you.

—"The God of Lost Things," Talis Kimberley

PART I

SOMETIMES THINGS GET LOST

1 FALLING BETWEEN THE CRACKS

THE FIRST THING ANTOINETTE Ricci ever lost was her father, but she was so young when it happened that she never really felt like she could be held responsible. She was only five years old, made of wiggles and giggles and still enough smaller than her name that no one ever called her anything other than "Antsy," not even her parents. She had never been hungry for longer than it took to tell an adult, never been hurt worse than a skinned knee or banged elbow, never truly been afraid.

It was a daddy-daughter day, something Antsy still viewed as a special treat, even though she knew that it was really to give her mother a few hours of peace after a long week of raising her hyperactive child. Mommy was going to go back to work as soon as Antsy started first grade, but until then, it was just the two of them all day while Daddy was at work, and that meant Saturdays were for Daddy and Antsy, Antsy and Daddy, just the two of them out in the world.

That was normal. That was right. That was the way things were supposed to be. And one minute he was there, watching indulgently from the end of the aisle as she ran wild and gleeful past ranks of Disney princesses and their jewel-toned plastic accessories, and then he wasn't there anymore. Antsy stopped running right in the middle of the aisle, too confused to move. Her parents *never* left her alone when they were at Target. That was one of their first and firmest rules; she could be allowed to free-range through the toys as long as she could see them,

but she couldn't let them slip out of sight, not ever, because the
world was full of people who wanted to snatch up pretty little
girls and walk away with them.

But her father—her tall, strong, broad-shouldered father
with the hair as bright a red as hers—wasn't there anymore.
He should have been right there at the end of the aisle, watching her with the little smile on his face that he reserved for
what he called her "feral child moments," what he called the
times when she ran wild and free and unfettered by the expec-
tations of a world that was inevitably going to come crashing
down on her soon enough.

Instead of her father, there was a pair of scuffed brown shoes
that stuck out just past the edge of the aisle. They looked familiar. She'd seen them at home, in the hall. Suddenly gripped
by the cold hand of caution, Antsy crept closer. Why were her
father's shoes on the floor? Where was her father? Grownups
didn't lay down on the floor the way kids sometimes did. They
were too tall. When they did get down on the floor to look
at something neat, they complained the whole time, saying
things that didn't make any sense, like "ow, my back" and
"when's the last time we vacuumed this carpet?" So her father
couldn't be wearing his shoes anymore, because he wouldn't
lay down like that, but the toes were pointed at the ceiling, and
shoes only did that when there were feet inside them.

She slowed down before she reached the shoes, before
she could see the person—not her father, it couldn't be her
father—who was wearing them. Something was very wrong.
If he'd been playing hide-seek without telling her, he would
already have popped back out to give her a chance to find
him, and if he wasn't, he'd never have left her alone like this.
She didn't want to reach the end of the aisle. She was suddenly
gripped by the unkind conviction that if she did, everything

was going to change, and she didn't want it to. She didn't want it to change at all. She had everything she wanted.

She had a nice room with a bunk bed that was just for her, and walls painted her favorite shade of green, with yellow daisies stenciled all around the baseboards. She'd helped with the daisies, and her handprint was pressed next to the doorframe, smaller than her hands were now, but still enough to make it clear that the room was *hers,* the space belonged to *her,* and no one was welcome there unless she wanted them to be.

She had a pretty mother with long dark hair and a laugh like watermelon on a hot summer afternoon, sweet and good and oddly sticky in its own way. Her mother's laughter *stuck* to you, and it made everything better for hours and hours, even after it was over. And she had the best father in the world, with red hair like her own, although he had a lot less of it—he'd started losing his hair before she was born, and when she'd seen pictures of him from the wedding and before, where his whole shiny skull was covered up by untamed red frizzes, she'd been scared of losing her own hair for more than a week, until her mother told her that because her hair was curly like Aunt Sally's and not straight like Daddy's, it wasn't going to happen. Her father didn't laugh as good as her mother did, but he knew the best games, and he was always happy to play them with her. He didn't mind mud or mess or spending hours at Target while she ran around and looked at all the toys.

She loved both her parents, and she loved her life, and she didn't want to lose any of it. She had the vague feeling that sometimes good things were only as good as they were because all the pieces had managed to line up *just so,* and if you took any of them away, it wouldn't be good anymore. Maybe not good at all.

So she stood frozen a few feet from the end of the aisle, staring at her father's shoes and trying to fight back the panic that threatened to rise up and overwhelm her. Something was wrong.

The feeling that something was wrong only grew when an unfamiliar adult voice asked, sharp and interrogative, "Sir? Sir, are you all right? Do you need me to call for—oh my God. *Someone call 911!*"

Not entirely sure what was happening, only that she was scared and alone and wanted her father, Antsy finally rushed forward the last few steps, until she could see, and stopped again, eyes going so wide that it hurt. She couldn't close them. She couldn't look away.

There were her father's shoes, toes pointed at the ceiling because they were still on her father's feet, and there was her father, flat on his back on the cold linoleum, staring up at the ceiling the way he always said *she* shouldn't do, because the lights would hurt her eyes. There was a woman she didn't know kneeling next to him and yelling, her fingers pressed against the side of his neck. Antsy's stomach seized up like a fist. She didn't think it was okay for this lady to be touching her father.

But he wasn't smacking the lady's hand away or telling her it was rude to touch people without permission. He wasn't doing anything. He wasn't even blinking.

People needed to blink. Blinking was *important*. Antsy sniffled.

The woman hadn't noticed her yet. She was looking over her shoulder and shouting something Antsy couldn't quite hear. There was a weird ringing sound in her ears, getting louder and louder the longer she looked at her father, still and silent and staring at the lights, unmoving on the Target floor.

She didn't even notice when her own throat hitched and she started keening, the sound high and horrible and inhuman. The woman's head snapped back around, taking in the crying child and the fact that her hair matched the dead man's in an instant, before she got to her feet and moved to put herself between the little girl and the body. "Oh, sweetheart," she said. "Don't look at that. No, no, don't look at that. Sweetheart, look at me."

Antsy tried to duck around the woman, who grabbed her by the shoulders and stopped her before she could complete the motion. "My name isn't *sweetheart* I don't *know* you you're not allowed to *touch* me I want my daddy!" Her voice peaked in a wail so high and sharp that it made the people in earshot wince.

And there were more of them than there had been only a few seconds before. People were pouring into their location, other shoppers and staffers in their familiar red Target vests. Antsy recognized one of them, the nice man who always restocked the Barbies when they'd been picked over. She'd asked him before if he knew where a specific toy was, and he had always been willing to help her find what she needed.

Wrenching herself away from the woman, she flung herself at the man and wrapped her arms around his leg, holding on tightly as she wailed. The man looked around helplessly, holding his hands up and well away from her.

"I didn't touch her," he said, voice gone defensive. "She grabbed on to me."

"Make Daddy wake up!" demanded Antsy, as if being an employee of Target gave him some sort of secret superpower.

"I can't, sweetheart, I'm sorry," he said. "I just stock the toys, I don't raise the—I'm sorry."

Antsy sniffled and wiped her face on the leg of his pants.

He patted her on the head like she was a puppy, tentative and still clearly half-afraid to touch her.

"'M Antsy," she said.

"David," he replied. "Is my name."

The woman who'd originally found her father was now talking earnestly to two men dressed as store security, gesturing alternately to the body and the child. Things got very hectic after that.

Someone pried Antsy off the man's leg. She started wailing again, and only wailed louder as EMTs and police officers arrived and loaded her father onto a gurney, wheeling him away. She tried to run after them, and a policewoman in a blue uniform stepped in front of her, kneeling down to look her in the eye.

"Where is your mother?" asked the policewoman.

Antsy sniffled, surprised enough to momentarily stop wailing and focus on the woman in front of her. "She says Target is daddy-daughter time," she said, voice thick with tears and snot, sounding younger than her five years. "Where are they taking my daddy?"

The policewoman's expression didn't change, remaining placid and a little sad. "Do you know your mother's phone number?" she asked. "We can call her together, if you know."

Antsy was still too young for a phone of her own, and so had been drilled on both her parents' numbers, in case they were ever separated. She sniffled, nodded, and recited the number she had never had cause to use like this before, even after all her mother's dire warnings.

The rest of that day was a blur, bright and terrible and unbearable, and the only mercy it held was that so little of it would stay in her memory, which seemed to have been blasted into shards by the image of her father's open eyes staring at the lights.

After that, whenever it was time for shopping, if shopping meant Target, Antsy would refuse to go inside. She would throw tantrums a toddler would be proud of, would scream and bite and kick and, once, even wet herself rather than be dragged through the doors. It didn't matter. She couldn't go inside, couldn't go under those lights, couldn't enter the air-conditioned aisles. It wasn't possible.

That was the day she lost her father. It would be years before she realized losing him had taken something less tangible and less provably important away at the same time: the feeling of safety and security in the world, like it was a kind place.

Memory came back in time for the funeral. They lowered him into the ground, and she stood next to her mother in a black dress—she'd never been allowed to have a black dress before, not even when she asked for it, black dresses were for sad people and she was supposed to be a happy little girl, and she couldn't even feel special and pretty, because her father wasn't there, he wasn't there, he was never going to be there again—and she didn't cry. All her tears had been spilled first in the toy aisles of Target and then the lobby of the police station where she'd been taken to wait for her mother, and as she got older, she would come to think that the ability to cry was the third thing she'd lost in a single day.

One thing could happen to anyone. Two things was a tragedy. Three things felt like carelessness. And for the rest of her life, she would remember that black dress and that solemn graveside, and going home after to put on jeans and a T-shirt and run around the backyard trying to pretend her father would be there when she went back inside the house, and her mother wouldn't look so sad, and her grandmother wouldn't be sitting on the couch crying like she had to make up for every tear Antsy herself couldn't shed.

After a week had passed, Antsy went back to school, finding herself suddenly a member of a small, involuntarily exclusive club for children with dead parents. People who had always been friendly toward her treated her like she had something contagious, like she had become an entirely different person over the span of a week and a half. Like a father having a massive heart attack in the toy section of Target was somehow catching.

Life went back to normal. Bit by bit, the color came back into the world, and Antoinette resumed living up to her nickname, always in motion, a little moving missile of red curls and laughter, full of fuss and bother. They called her "Antsy" not just because it was shorter than her given name, and not just because there was a girl in her class named "Anne" but because she was never still for more than a few seconds. Her tendency to squirm during class had gotten her into trouble more than once, and her teacher felt bad for having appreciated her stillness during the days right after her father's funeral.

Life not only went back to normal: life went on. New things happened, things her father had never been a part of, and shortly after Antsy's sixth birthday, the new thing that happened was a man in her living room, a man named Tyler who held her mother's hand and watched Antsy with heavy-lidded eyes, studying her in a way that made her feel like she was something he was thinking about buying from the store and not a little girl in her own home, with a mother who loved her and a father who was lost, but not on purpose.

Antsy didn't like him. She didn't like to be alone with him, but she couldn't say the right reasons why, couldn't find them in her lists of good reasons not to like or want or enjoy a thing. It wasn't that he was a man who wasn't related to her—only the fact that she liked David from the toy aisle as much as she did had let her try going back to Target with her mother the first time, and that was the only time she'd been able to make it past the doors before she fled to the parking lot in tears, pursued by her worried, mortified mother. And it wasn't that the man was in her house. Lots of people had been in her house since her father died, relatives she didn't really know and neighbors with casseroles and condolences. She couldn't say *why* she didn't like him, only that she didn't, not one little bit, and it didn't matter, because her mother didn't seem to see it. He came around more and more often, first every other weekend and then every single one, and then during the week, too, so that sometimes she'd come home from school and he'd be there already.

Then one day she came home and he was there and her mother wasn't, and they were alone together for the very first time. Antsy froze, going still in a way her teachers would never have believed she was capable of, and stared at him in solemn-eyed silence until he frowned and left the living room for the kitchen, leaving her alone. She fled for her bedroom immediately, shutting the door as hard as she could and throwing herself onto the bottom bunk of her bed, not sure *why* she was so upset, only that she was.

There was so much she didn't seem to know. It was like her father had taken all the answers with him when he left, and now she had to live in a world that didn't have any answers in it at all.

She lay on her bed and shivered until she heard her mother's car in the driveway. Only then did she relax enough to fall asleep, and when her mother woke her for dinner, Tyler was still there. He sat at their table in the place where her father was supposed to be, and he put the potatoes on her plate like they were a gift, like the meal her mother had cooked in their very own kitchen was something he had the power and authority to bestow. Antsy ate in silence, and if her mother thought that was strange at all, she didn't say so.

The next day, when Antsy got home, Tyler wasn't there, but her mother was there, waiting for her. She took Antsy by the hand and led her to the couch, and then she talked to her the way adults talked to children when they wanted them to agree to something that wasn't ever a question, not really. She said words like "lonely" and "difficult" and "without your father," and Antsy listened in frozen silence that felt too big to break, and when her mother finished on a question, she didn't hear it at first. It was too much: it was too big. She couldn't force it down.

Her mother frowned and squeezed her hand. "Sweetheart, did you hear me? Were you listening?"

The woman at Target had called her "sweetheart," too, called her "sweetheart" while standing to block the shape of Antsy's father's body, and that word felt like poison in her ears. She flinched away, suddenly scowling.

"I was listening," she said. "I'm sorry. Can I go to my room?"

"I need you to answer me, please, and then you can go and play."

Antsy didn't want to go and play, and she didn't know what her mother had asked. The ringing in her ears was back, taking all the sound in the world away. So she just looked at her mother, trying to understand the movement of her lips as she looked Antsy gravely in the eye and repeated her question:

"Tyler has asked me to marry him, and I told him I can't unless you say it's all right. So is it all right, Antoinette? May I marry the man who loves me?"

This time the words got through, despite the veil of static. Antsy swallowed hard, forcing fear and revulsion away, and looked her mother dead in the eye as she said, "I don't like him."

"He's not trying to replace your father, baby girl. No one's ever going to do that. But it's hard to be a parent all by myself, and I'm lonely. He'll be your friend, if you'll let him."

Antsy still didn't know why she didn't like the man who seemed to make her mother so happy—happy enough that she'd do this, happy enough that she'd change the shape of their family this way. So she bit her lip, and held her silence long enough that her mother started to look anxious and unhappy, and finally said, "If you want to marry him, I guess it's okay."

Her mother laughed and smiled and put her arms around her, gathering her into a hug. "Thank you, baby. Thank you so much. You're not going be sorry about this, you're not."

But Antsy, who was already sorry about her answer, said nothing.

2 EVERYTHING CHANGES

LATER, WHEN ANTSY WAS far enough removed from the moment to look at the timeline, she would realize Tyler had asked her mother to marry him six months after her father's funeral, almost to the day, and the wedding was set for three months after that. It was a brief courtship by any reasonable standard, brief enough to raise more than a few eyebrows. Not that it stopped them: by the time she was due to start first grade, Antsy had a new last name, a new stepfather, and a new permanent resident in her home.

She had been the flower girl at their wedding, dressed in a white-and-pink confection of a dress with a skirt that swirled around her calves and capped sleeves that ringed her upper arms in lace and a basket full of pink and white rose petals, and everyone who'd come to see her mother married had made happy noises of contentment when they saw her, like her participation in the ceremony was somehow the proof that it hadn't been too quick, that her father would have wanted the love of his life to move on and be happy in his absence, like everything was okay.

After the wedding, she had gone to stay with her grandparents for a week while her mother and her new husband spent some adult time at a nice local hotel. Antsy had spent the entire time running wild in the backyard or the park or the living room or the grocery store, whatever fields she was offered for her feral thrashings, and she had never allowed herself to give voice to the fact that she didn't like her new stepfather, had never told anyone but her mother, who had been entirely unwilling to hear her.

That was the fourth thing she lost: the belief that if something made her unhappy or uncomfortable, she could tell an adult who loved her and they would make everything better. Her mother hadn't listened, and now they were married. Married was forever, unless you got divorced, and from the way most of the kids she knew talked about divorced, that was one of the worst things in the whole world. She didn't want to wish something bad on her mother, not after everything she'd been through already, and so even though she didn't like the man who was now her stepfather, she wasn't going to hope her mother divorced him.

At least, she wasn't going to do it where anyone could hear her.

So she ran and ran and ran, like she could run fast enough to run all the way back to the afternoon in Target where her father fell down and didn't get back up again, and when the week ended without time reversing itself, she went home, to the bedroom that had always been her sanctuary, to a new toothbrush on the bathroom sink and a new body at the dinner table.

Tyler had been around a lot in the months leading up to the wedding, but after, it seemed like he was never gone, like every time she turned around he was *there*. He ate dinner with them. When they went to the park, he drove the car, and when they went to the movies, he sat on her mother's other side, holding her hand, stealing her popcorn. He was *there*, whether or not she wanted him to be. In her home, all the time, whenever she turned around.

And she still didn't like him, and she still didn't know why. At Christmas, when they did their school talent show and she looked out to see him sitting with her mother in the audience, another kid from her class said, "There's your new daddy, Antsy," and the wave of rage she felt was almost a relief. She didn't like him because he was trying to take her father's place. That was all. That was a completely reasonable and understandable reason not to like someone she barely knew, and if her mother asked again why she didn't like Tyler, she'd have an answer.

She sang beautifully that night and went home smiling. She still didn't like Tyler, not one bit, but now she felt like she understood *why,* and understanding a thing was the first step toward conquering it.

She could learn to like him, if she knew why she didn't. She ate dinner and she kissed her mother on the cheek and she nodded to Tyler and she went to bed, and everything was going to be fine.

Two things happened that weekend. Her mother sat down with her on the couch, the same way she'd done on the day she said she wanted to marry Tyler, but this time she was smiling like the sunrise, like she had the best secret in the whole world. So her mother wasn't going to ask for her permission to get divorced, then, if that was the sort of thing that mothers asked for permission to do. Antsy didn't know. She hadn't known mothers asked permission to get married in the first place, so *would* her mother ask for permission to stop being married?

Instead, her mother took her hands and said, that sunrise smile melting into a look of profound seriousness, "Sweetie, you're going to be a big sister. Tyler and I are going to have a baby."

Antsy frowned. Antsy tilted her head. "I don't understand," she said.

"Well, honey, I'm pregnant."

"But why would that make me a big sister?" she asked. "Tyler's not my daddy."

Her mother frowned, the sort of frown that started with her eyes and made a furrow between her brows, so she looked sad and disappointed all at once, like she didn't know how to swallow the rock she'd just been handed. "Tyler is your stepfather," she said. "He's never going to replace your father, but he's not going anywhere. You'll have time to learn how to love him. Maybe he'll be your daddy someday, and since I'm your mommy now, and this baby is going to be my baby, too, that means they're going to be your family just as soon as they're born. They're already your family."

Antsy had never been particularly interested in being a big sister. The kids in her class who had little brothers and sisters mostly seemed to view them as unwanted complications rather than the guaranteed friends the adults in their lives always tried to paint them as. Little kids grew into bigger kids, and bigger kids could be fun to play with, but little ones were sticky and loud and unpredictable in ways that didn't make any sense, because making sense wasn't a thing they knew how to care about yet.

At six, Antsy was old enough that the wild illogic of infancy and toddlerhood was starting to fade into hazy memory. She wouldn't be able to understand a baby. She wouldn't be able to reason with them. "No, thank you," she said politely.

Her mother squeezed her hands tighter. "I don't think you understand," she said. "I'm having a baby. It's not something you get to agree or disagree with, it's something that's happening, right here and right now."

Antsy's eyes grew wide and alarmed. "You're having a baby *now?*" she squeaked. She had seen pregnant women before. They had hard, round bellies, not soft and squishy like her teacher, Mrs. Baker, who she absolutely and entirely adored, and who had laughed and said, "No, honey, I'm just fat," the one time a student had asked her if she was going to have a baby. Pregnant women were so full of baby that they looked like they had swallowed a whole watermelon the way her class corn snake swallowed mice, putting the entire thing inside themselves, rind and all. Her mother didn't look like that, didn't look pregnant in any way that she could recognize.

To her relief, her mother shook her head. "No," she said. "I'm having a baby in about six months. I just wanted you to know before I told anyone else."

"Not even Tyler?"

"Except for Tyler. He's my husband now, sweetheart. When I learn something important, he's the first person I tell."

Hearing it said—not just implied but *said*—that Tyler was more important than she was made Antsy's stomach sink all the way down to the bottom of her toes. She nodded slowly, tugging her hands away. "Can I go to my room now?"

"Of course, darling. Thank you for letting me tell you my big news. It's not for public yet, so please don't tell your grandparents."

Antsy had never kept a secret from her grandparents before. Oh, there were things she didn't tell them—they didn't know about all the games she played at school, or all the things she did with her Barbies, or every time she used the bathroom— but she'd never been told something and then asked specifically not to share it. She blinked, trying to incorporate this new piece of information into her ideas of the way the world worked. Adults could ask her to keep things from other adults.

Antsy frowned, uneasy. "All right," she said. "I won't tell them. I'm going to my room."

Her mother nodded and let her go, and she didn't realize

that by telling Antsy to keep a secret from two of the people she trusted most in the world, she had just broken something small, and fragile, and irreparable. When Antsy made the lists of things she'd lost, to justify being Lost herself, she didn't include her belief that adults could be trusted. That thing, out of everything, had been so small and fundamental that she couldn't even see that it was gone.

But ah, narrative can be confusing at times. It carries forward, regardless of the reader, action creating consequence, consequence creating story, and you may have forgotten that two things happened this weekend. You can't be blamed if you did. Some things are better to forget.

That night, after dinner had been eaten and the dishes washed and put away, snug in their clean, closed cupboards, Antsy went to her room to sit on the floor and play Barbies, as she so often did in the evenings. But unlike most nights, she had been in there for less than an hour before there was a knock at her bedroom door. She looked up, curious, and called, "Come in, Mom!"

But when the door opened, it wasn't her mother on the other side. Instead, Tyler slipped into her room, which had previously been a sort of sacred space for her, the one place in the house not yet impacted by his implacable presence. Antsy recoiled before she could stop herself, every muscle in her body tensing and remaining tense as he closed the door behind himself and walked over to the bed, settling on the edge of the mattress.

"Your mother told me she told you that we're expecting a baby," he said, without attempt at preamble. "I know this all has to be a lot, and very quickly, for you. I'm sorry about that. Change is always hard. At least all the change is happening at once? I handle things better when they don't draw themselves out."

"I don't," said Antsy. She was starting to feel that change was like cookies. One a night would be wonderful, but if you ate too many at one time, you'd wind up making yourself sick and not getting any cookies for a week.

She felt a little sick. Having Tyler in her room, sitting on her bed, didn't help. She quietly decided that she'd be sleeping in the upper bunk tonight, and every night until it was time to change her sheets again. She didn't want to sleep where he'd been sitting.

Slow horror grew in her belly when he patted the mattress beside himself. "Come over here," he said. "I want to talk to you."

Antsy didn't move. Tyler frowned, just a little, and patted the mattress again.

"I don't bite, Antoinette," he said. "Come over here."

Antsy didn't like him. She didn't like the way he touched her mother or the way he looked at Antsy herself, or the way he insisted on using her full name all the time, like everything he said was too important to be anchored to a nickname. But she knew she was supposed to get along with people and be fair to them, even when she didn't like them, and since it wasn't Tyler's fault that her daddy was gone, it didn't seem fair to keep on punishing him being there and loving her mother when her daddy couldn't. She was supposed to be a good girl. She was supposed to be nice, and kind, and all the other things little girls are told to be.

And her daddy was never coming back, not ever, and her mother hadn't been as sad since Tyler came to live with them. He wasn't helping Antsy the same way, but he wasn't hurting her, either. It would hurt her mother if she didn't at least try to get along with him, since he was a part of their family now and was always going to be.

Antsy pushed herself off the floor and approached the bed with the cautious hesitancy of a wounded animal, finally settling next to Tyler on the mattress. He put his hand on her leg, keeping her from pulling away.

"This baby is going to be your little brother or sister," he said gravely. "It's a very big responsibility to be a big sister, and I know you're going to do a wonderful job."

"How is it a responsibility?" asked Antsy warily. She knew girls her own age who had little brothers and sisters at home, who were expected to spend all their time taking care of babies when they weren't in school, feeding them and changing their diapers and making sure they didn't hurt themselves on a world that seemed designed entirely of things meant for hurting babies. She liked playing with her dolls. She found the idea of playing with a living doll that screamed and peed and spit up and couldn't be left face-down in the yard when she got tired of it a lot less appealing.

"You're going to have to be the one who teaches them what's right and wrong, and how to take care of their toys and what ice cream is."

"Oh." Antsy liked that better than she liked the idea of diapers and bottles. "I guess I can do that."

"Good. I'm glad you're on board with this." He squeezed her leg before finally taking his hand away. Antsy was almost ashamed of how relieved she was. "Your mother's very excited about this baby, and so am I. It would be wonderful if you could find it in you to be excited with us."

"I'll try," said Antsy honestly. "It's still very new. I didn't know there would be a baby."

"Neither did your mother," said Tyler, and put his hand back on her leg, squeezing it again before standing, a smile on his mustachioed face.

The place where his hand had been felt hot, like she'd been pressing a heated towel against it. Antsy stayed where she was and watched as Tyler made his way to the door, pausing with his hand on the doorknob to smile indulgently back at her.

"Thank you for talking to me," he said. "Goodnight, bug. Sleep well."

Then he was gone, and Antsy was alone. She changed into her nightgown, quickly, and climbed up to the top bunk of her bed, shivering as she crawled under the covers. It was a long time before she fell asleep, but she didn't even stir when her mother came in to tell her to brush her teeth. It was unusual enough for Antsy to go to bed early that her mother looked at the sleeping child for a long moment before she frowned and let her be.

She could talk to Antsy about the way she was reacting to the idea of a baby in the morning.

3 EVERYTHING FALLS APART

THUS BEGAN WHAT ANYONE looking in from the outside would probably have assumed was one of the most exciting times in Antsy's life. Her mother finally told her own parents she was expecting a baby, almost two whole weeks after telling Antsy, and they couldn't have been happier for her. Antsy wondered sometimes if that had something to do with her grandma being her mother's mother and not her father's; her father's mother was much less enthusiastic when they finally called her to give her the news.

Antsy had never been particularly close to her paternal grandmother, but in that moment, she felt like they were the only two members of the family who understood each other. She would have crossed the country to join her in her small, safe apartment in Manhattan, if she'd been able to figure out how to do it.

She was trying as hard as she could, trying every single day, and it made her happy to see her mother so happy: her mother's friends liked to say that she was glowing, and while she wasn't—she didn't light up a room in any way other than the ordinary ones—she was smiling more, happy and healthy and beautiful, even as her belly grew larger and more pronounced by the day. Antsy wanted to be excited about the impending baby, but she couldn't figure out quite how.

It didn't help that now, with a baby coming, all the kids in her class whose parents had gotten divorced and remarried liked to tell her about how Tyler was *never* going to leave. Sometimes they seemed unnaturally gleeful about her presumed future unhappiness. Once the new parent made a baby with the existing parent, that was it. They were there forever.

Antsy didn't want Tyler to be there forever. She wasn't even sure she wanted him to be there for now. The more time passed with nothing bad happening, the more unreasonable her dislike of the man felt, but she still called him by name, and she still refused when her mother tried to nudge them, however gently, toward finding their own version of her much-missed daughter-daddy trips to Target. She didn't like the idea of being alone with him even more than she didn't like the way he looked at her sometimes.

She still didn't have the words to explain *why* she didn't like those things, just the slow and septic understanding that it wasn't about him trying to replace her daddy, and that she didn't, couldn't, wouldn't learn to like them. They were a part of who Tyler was, and as long as she could make nice well enough to let him be a part of their family, did it really matter if she *liked* the man? She didn't like broccoli, either, but she ate it when it was on her plate, not like peppers. She hated peppers so, so much that her mother didn't even cook with them anymore.

Antsy didn't hate Tyler, not yet, and maybe not ever. And he was kind to her mother as her belly grew bigger, bringing her drinks, rubbing her feet, doing more and more of the grocery shopping and driving Antsy to school like there had never been any question that he'd be willing to do those things.

It was about a month before the baby was born when things got really bad for the first time.

Antsy's mother had been feeling icky all day. Her head hurt and her back hurt and her ankles hurt and her list of things that hurt was so long and detailed it seemed like every part of her must be in pain. Antsy was afraid to ask any questions about it, because what if she said her *hair* hurt? That would be a horror beyond all understanding or accepting. Antsy wouldn't be able to handle hearing that from her mother, so it was better not to ask. She had been sitting at the table, placidly coloring a picture of a unicorn in a field all full of flowers, when she smelled hamburger frying in a pan. She looked up, and then behind herself. Her mother was still stretched on the couch, her belly jutting up like a boulder, a warm washcloth on her forehead.

Antsy turned, slowly, to look toward the kitchen. The smell of hamburger continued, and she could hear faint sizzling sounds. Someone was cooking.

Carefully, she put down her crayons and slid out of her seat, padding silently toward the kitchen and peeking inside. There was Tyler, standing over the stove with a spatula in his hand, stirring something. She must have made a sound, because he turned and smiled at the sight of her.

"Let your mother know dinner's handled," he said. "And if you'd set the table, that would be fantastic."

His tone made it clear that he wasn't actually asking. Antsy was used to setting the table for dinner. She nodded solemnly and moved to begin collecting plates, taking herself farther into the room. She usually did her best to avoid being alone in a room with Tyler, but this was a specific task, and if there was a way to set the table without getting dishes down from the cabinet, she didn't know what it would be.

"No," he said sharply, as she was pulling down plates. "Not those plastic things. *Real* plates."

Antsy froze. She wasn't allowed to carry the grown-up plates on her own. She was too prone to dropping things. She wasn't a particularly clumsy child, but she was still a child, and a fidgety one at that. All children will drop things, fidgety children more than most.

But Tyler was looking at her with a frown, and she thought maybe he didn't know she wasn't allowed to touch the real plates. Even if he *did* know, she didn't know how to argue with him. Throat tight, Antsy replaced the sturdy plastic plates they always used for dinner, giving one of them a small pat of apology, before reaching for the forbidden plates behind them. They were hefty ceramic, weathered and chipped from endless trips through the dishwasher, and while they weren't unfamiliar, they also weren't for every day. She counted out three and carried them, with precarious caution, out of the kitchen to the table.

"Tyler says he's got dinner handled," she said, feeling very grown-up as she set the real plates on the table. They made a little clinking sound, which the plastic ones never did, and she puffed her chest out with pride, because she hadn't dropped a single one.

Her mother sat up at the sound, eyes going wide. "Antoinette Richards-Ricci, did you touch the good plates?" she demanded.

Antsy froze at the tone of her mother's voice, and finally said, "Tyler told me to."

"You know better than to touch the good plates," said her mother. "You should have told him no."

Antsy didn't know what to do. Her mother and father used to fight sometimes, but they had never used her to do it; any disagreements they had about parenting had been conducted while she was in another room, out of earshot. "I'm . . . I'm . . ." she managed, before ducking her head and scuttling for the kitchen. Maybe if she finished setting the table, her mother wouldn't be so angry. Maybe forks and napkins were a talisman against maternal wrath.

Tyler looked up and frowned when she came running in. "Slow down," he said. "It's not a race."

"Do we, um, do we need knives tonight? Or just forks?"

"How do you like your Sloppy Joes?" he asked.

Antsy didn't know what a Sloppy Joes was. She blinked at him, bewildered and a little wild-eyed, still trying to process the fact that her mother was mad at her for doing what she'd been told to do. "Um," she said finally. "With a . . . fork?" Saying she didn't want a knife was usually safe, especially when her mother was already in a rotten mood.

"That's fine," he said, and she dove for the silverware drawer with relief, pulling it open and getting out three forks before picking up a short stack of napkins and heading back into the dining room.

Her mother had reached the table and was scowling at the mess of Antsy's crayons and coloring pages, which she hadn't had the time to clear away yet. Antsy put the forks and napkins down, not taking the time to line them up just so in her hurry to clear her things off the table.

"You should have cleaned this up before you started," said her mother, settling in her chair. Then she thawed slightly, saying, "I'm sorry, pumpkin. I appreciate you stepping up and helping Tyler with dinner. It's very kind of you."

"I didn't know Tyler knew how to cook," said Antsy. "I thought if you didn't feel good enough to do it, we'd have pizza."

"I can cook a few things," said Tyler, emerging from the kitchen to kiss her mother on the temple as he put a large bowl of salad down on the table. "Antoinette, go get the glasses."

She didn't like that word. "You mean the cups?" she asked, hopefully.

Tyler frowned. "Why would I have said 'the glasses' when I meant 'the cups'?"

"Because Antsy still isn't allowed to carry the glasses by herself," said her mother sternly. "So you must have meant cups."

"Oh," said Tyler. "Yes, I meant cups."

Antsy skittered back into the kitchen before he could change his mind again, returning with three brightly colored plastic tumblers. She set one in front of each place setting, then slid into her own chair, still feeling unreasonably proud of herself for carrying the plates without dropping them, even if it might have been better if she'd told Tyler no. He probably hadn't realized she wasn't supposed to.

She froze when she realized both Tyler and her mother were looking at her. Swallowing hard, she asked, "Did I do something wrong?"

"Tyler didn't tell you to get the good plates," said her mother. "Why would you make up something like that?"

"I wouldn't! I mean, I didn't. I mean, he did so." Antsy looked at Tyler like he might change his mind about whatever lie he'd told her mother and tell her the truth. "I started to get the plates I'm supposed to use, and he told me to get the other ones."

Tyler looked at her, an expression of exaggerated disappointment on his face. "I knew you didn't like me, but this isn't nice of you," he said, and walked back to the kitchen, leaving her to gape after him, mouth moving silently.

Her mother sighed. "Antsy, I wish you'd try to get along with your stepfather," she said. "I wish you'd make an effort. This baby will be here soon, and I'm going to need you to step way, way up around here."

Antsy had long since figured out that "big responsibility"

didn't just mean teaching the baby fun things, even if she wasn't expected to change diapers or wipe noses. Her mother couldn't do a lot of her own chores since she'd gotten too big to bend over, and somehow this always translated to Antsy doing them, even when they were things she'd never done before, like dusting or trying to run the vacuum, and never to Tyler doing them.

He mowed the lawn and he took out the trash and he did the grocery shopping, and somehow that was enough. But she'd been stepping up this whole time. She frowned at her mother. "Like how?" she asked.

"Cleaning the bathrooms," said her mother.

Antsy blinked. "But I did, this weekend," she said.

"Please don't lie to me again," said her mother. "I know Tyler did it."

Antsy stared at her for a moment before she walked around the table and sat, folding her hands in her lap like she'd been taught to do when she was the first one to dinner. She could tell when arguing wasn't going to do her any good, and this was one of those times. Her mother had that thin line between her eyebrows that meant she wasn't all the way listening anymore, because she already knew Antsy wasn't going to tell her the truth. Better not to bother.

Silent, Antsy looked down at her hands until she heard Tyler come out of the kitchen, carrying a jug of milk in one hand and a serving platter of what looked like hamburgers in the other. He set them down, then returned to the kitchen, returning a second time with a big salad bowl and a plate of tater tots.

"Everybody dig in," he said, sitting and dishing a healthy amount of salad and one of the sort-of hamburgers onto his own plate.

Antsy's mother did the same, smiling at Tyler the whole time. "Thank you for fixing dinner," she said. "Everything looks wonderful. Antsy, don't just take tater tots. You have to eat some salad."

Antsy nodded and reached for the bowl but stopped before she touched it, pulling her hand away. "I can't," she said.

Her mother frowned, eyes narrowing. "What do you mean, you can't?"

"It has peppers all in it," said Antsy.

"It's been what, a year since you tried eating one? A lot can change in a year," said her mother. "Maybe you like peppers now. Take some salad."

Antsy made a face but scooped some salad onto her plate. She could always eat around the peppers to make her mother happy. Then she took one of the weird hamburger things. It smelled sort of like spaghetti smelled, and it was dripping. It looked like Tyler had just made a thick spaghetti sauce and put it on a bun. Why did that need a special name?

Tyler waited until they all had some of everything and milk in their cups before picking up his own burger-thing and taking a big bite. Antsy had learned to wait until at least one of the adults was eating, to keep herself from finishing too far ahead of everyone else. She picked up her Sloppy Joe and took a tentative bite.

Then she froze, the hated, revolting taste of peppers coating her tongue. Tyler was looking at her like he was daring her to spit it out. She saw a trap snapping shut in his expression, baited with her carrying the forbidden plates and primed by his lying to her mother. She couldn't understand what it was supposed to do; she just knew she didn't like it. Antsy put the Sloppy Joe carefully back on the plate and took a big gulp of milk, washing the single bite she'd taken down her throat.

"I'm sorry my head hurts can I please be excused?" she said, all a rush, with no pauses to breathe or choose a better path through the sentence.

Her mother blinked and sat up a little straighter, suddenly focused on her daughter. "Are you all right?"

"She's just trying to make sure she doesn't get in trouble for using the wrong plates," said Tyler. "She felt fine a minute ago."

If he could lie, so could she. "No, I didn't," said Antsy. "My head's been hurting all afternoon, but I didn't want to whine and make Mom worry when she doesn't feel good already, so I didn't say anything. But now it hurts worse because I can smell food, and if I eat my whole dinner, I'm afraid I'll be sick."

That was the best threat she had. Even with her mother unable to do most of her chores, Antsy had faith that she wouldn't want Antsy to clean up her own sick if she lost her dinner—and if she forced herself to keep eating peppers, she *would* lose her dinner. And Tyler wasn't going to clean up a little kid's sick, especially when that kid wasn't his own.

"You can go to your room," said her mother. "But only to your room. This isn't freedom to do whatever you want. No television, no dessert. We'll talk about the plates in the morning."

They would, too, if she remembered; Antsy could see the promise in the line between her mother's eyebrows, even as she could see the weariness that meant the conversation probably wouldn't happen. She certainly wasn't going to be the one to start it. She tried hard to be a good girl—always had and always would—but she was still a six-year-old being accused of something she hadn't done, and the longer she could avoid that trouble, the happier she would be.

Leaving her dinner, salad, and tater tots untouched, a single bite taken from her Sloppy Joe, Antsy rose from the table and crossed to peck her mother on the cheek and nod respectfully to Tyler. "Goodnight," she said.

"Clear your plate," snapped Tyler.

Antsy had been wondering whether he remembered how much she hated peppers when he was setting the menu for tonight. When she heard that tone in his voice, she had her answer. He'd done it on purpose, just like he'd ordered her to set the table with real plates on purpose. He was trying to get her into trouble. He wanted her mother to be angry with her, and her to be begging and pleading for her side of the story. She just couldn't figure out *why* a grownup would want to have a fight with a first-grader.

She also couldn't make it easier on him. That wasn't the sort of girl she was. So she looked him in the eye and said, "No."

Tyler inhaled, anger clearly growing, but before he could speak, her mother asked, in a weary but reasonable tone, "Why do you not want to do something an adult has asked you to do?"

"My head already hurts, and I'm more likely to drop things when my head hurts," Antsy said. "I don't want to risk dropping the plate and making a big mess someone else will have to clean up."

There: a good reason, sensible, and well within the limits of acceptability. Tyler settled back into his seat, still looking unhappy, and her mother managed a wan smile as she touched Antsy on the cheek.

"You're my good girl," she said. "Always so good. Always better than I deserved."

"I love you," said Antsy, and fled to her room. She emerged

half an hour later to brush her teeth, grimacing and touching her temples the whole time, and while she saw Tyler watching from the hallway, reflected in the bathroom mirror like an unfriendly ghost, no one tried to talk to her or interrupt her. Clean, hungry, and afraid, Antsy went to bed.

THE BABY CAME ON time, as babies sometimes will, and loudly, as babies always do. A girl, a baby sister. Tyler and her mother tucked the crib into their room, and Antsy sat rigid with silent fear as she realized what the baby's arrival really meant. She couldn't sleep with the little girl wailing in the next room, but she wasn't sleeping anyway, too afraid to close her eyes.

They named the baby Abigail. She became "Abby" instantly, even to Tyler, who still wouldn't call Antsy by any name but "Antoinette." And for a while, she took up all the attention in the house and all the air in whatever room she was in.

That was better. A Tyler focused on his daughter was a Tyler not looking at Antsy with that expression that made her skin crawl for reasons she couldn't understand; a Tyler who cared about the baby was a Tyler who didn't care about Antsy. She wanted that more than anything. She still didn't like him, and she still didn't know exactly why. He wasn't trying to be her daddy, but as to what he *was* trying to be, she couldn't say.

After that one bad dinner, he had never tried to play her against her mother like that again. Instead, he sat too close to her on the couch, he put his hands on her legs or arms whenever he had the slightest excuse, and he watched her.

Everywhere she went, he watched her. He watched her when she left for school, on the days when he hadn't already gone to work, and he watched her when she played in the backyard on the weekends. His eyes were a constant danger, far worse than his hands, which required her to lower her guard and get close enough to grab. She hated them so. Her dislike was taking root and sprouting thorns, becoming something wilder and more tangled.

Six months after Abby was born, her mother sat her down in the living room and took her hands, as she'd done twice before. Antsy sat rigid, having learned that these were the moments where her life changed for the worse, where things she didn't even know could be lost were ripped away from her and thrown aside. Somewhere in the time between her father's collapse and now, she realized, she had lost the belief that her mother would always protect her, and somehow that burned the worst of all.

"Sweetheart," said her mother. "This house isn't big enough for our whole family. You know that. The baby can't sleep with me and Tyler forever."

"So she can share my room with me," blurted Antsy, desperate to say something—say anything—that wouldn't let the next change leave her mother's lips. "I don't mind. I already have a bunk bed. She can have the bottom bunk while she's all little, and then when she gets bigger, we can take turns on top. It'll be fun. Like having a sleepover, but with a sister."

"Oh, darling, that's very generous of you, but it wouldn't be fair. This house isn't big enough, and it's full of memories that make us sadder than we have to be. Your father wouldn't want us to be sad."

Antsy wanted to scream. Her father wouldn't have wanted Tyler lurking in the hall and watching her brush her teeth. He wouldn't have wanted her to feel like she was being haunted in her own home, even though she didn't understand *why* she felt that way. And she thought that maybe if he'd been there, he wouldn't have wanted her to understand. She thought keeping her from ever understanding might have been the most important thing in the whole world to him.

"We're moving," said her mother.

Antsy stared at her, eyes large and grave and petrified. Her mother, weary and happy and unable to understand why she'd be alone in either of those things, squeezed her hands and smiled.

"You'll have a bigger yard and a better room and you'll never have to share it," she said. "It's going to be wonderful."

"Yes," parroted Antsy. "Wonderful."

PART II

WHERE THE LOST
THINGS GO

4 SOMETIMES THINGS MISPLACE THEMSELVES

THE NEW HOUSE WAS bigger, and filled with light, with windows in every room, and Antsy hated it and loved it at the same time, because more space meant more opportunities for Tyler to catch her alone, away from her mother, and more light meant fewer shadows for him to hide in.

It was almost a year after Abby's birth when Antsy heard her bedroom door swing open in what felt like the middle of the night and sat up with a gasp, clutching her blankets to her chest as she saw the man in the doorway. He was a shadow against shadows; all the windows in the world couldn't stop the sun from setting. He walked toward the bed. Antsy watched him come, eyes very wide, barely even daring to breathe.

He stopped only a few feet away, watching her. Taking her measure for something she didn't understand and didn't want to, and her vague discomfort and dislike finally solidified, becoming a hatred so thick it choked her, making it difficult to breathe. He had never *done* anything, apart from occasional attempts to make her fight with her mother; always little things, like the plates, or like swearing he'd told her they were leaving soon when she knew full well that he hadn't. Always his word against hers. And what she had learned, again and again, was that her mother would believe him every time. He was the adult, he was her husband, and Antsy was just a little girl who had never been fully accepting of his place in her life. She was the unreliable one, not him. Not *Tyler*.

But she was the one safe in her bed while Tyler was the one standing silently where he had no business being and staring at her like he expected something. Antsy finally shrank away.

"You can't be in here," she said. "You can't . . . you can't be *in* here. This is *my room*."

"And this is my house," he said. "I paid for it; I own it. So is this really your room, or is this the room I let you borrow as long as it's convenient for me?"

Antsy had never considered that her room might not actually belong to her, that it might be in some way conditional. She glared at Tyler. "It's mine," she said. "I chose the paint for the walls, and my *father* bought me this bed. This is my room."

"You know your mother will believe me if I tell her something and you tell her something else," said Tyler, and moved closer still, finally sitting on the edge of the bed. "You know I could make things a lot harder for you than they are right now."

Antsy did know those things. She continued to watch him, wound up and wary, almost too afraid to blink.

"I can also make them easier," he said. "I know you asked your mother for a bike. I could convince her it would be a good idea to let you have one. If I said I thought you'd make more friends in our new neighborhood if you could get around more easily, you know she'd listen to me. You and I don't have to be enemies."

"We don't?" whispered Antsy. She felt like it was important that this hadn't happened in their old house, in her old room, where her mother had been right across the hall, close enough to hear her if she yelled. Here, her mother was on a different floor of the house. She'd still come running if she heard Antsy scream, but she'd have to come up the stairs, and the noise would wake the baby, and her mother was still so tired all the time . . .

Suddenly, the extra size of the new house didn't feel like a way to avoid Tyler. It felt like the trap she'd seen that long-ago night at the dinner table, finally snapping shut around her.

"We could be friends," said Tyler, and reached over, and unfastened the top button of her nightgown. That was all. Just one button, just one little twist of his fingers, and then he was standing, the smile on his face visible even through the dimness of the room around him. "Think about it, and remember: if you tell your mother anything, I'll tell her you're a liar, and she'll believe me. Not you. Me. Goodnight, Antoinette."

Those words were the final crack in the wall between her and the crying she had lost when her father died. Tyler let himself out of the room as the first fat, slow tears began to roll down her cheeks and her shoulders began to shake, and she finally understood why she'd never liked him, why the way he looked at her had always felt like a hand running along her spine, why having him in her house was an endless offense to the way the world was supposed to work.

But she also knew her mother wouldn't listen if she tried to tell her what she was afraid of, knew it with the bone-deep conviction that children can sometimes bring to things that are entirely untrue. She knew Santa Claus wasn't real; his handwriting had changed when her father died, and that had been the last piece of a puzzle she'd been unwillingly assembling for over a year. She still believed in the Tooth Fairy, and the Easter Bunny, and the mystical power of cracks to snap the spines of mothers. She believed so many things that weren't true that one more would have made no real difference if it hadn't been for the nature of this final, brutal, unendurable thing.

Tyler had been careful to demonstrate, over and over again, that when it was her word against his, he was the trustworthy adult and she was the child making up stories to get attention or avoid getting into trouble for whatever reason. He'd given her a lesson to learn, and she had learned it well. Too well to see how false and cruel it was, to understand that had she gone to her mother, her mother, who had a better understanding of the world and all its dangers, would have taken her side.

Still crying, Antsy slipped out of bed and—after checking her door to be sure it was all the way closed—stripped out of her nightgown, putting on the clothes she'd worn the day before, that were still at the top of the laundry basket. She was seven years old, almost eight, and she knew she should get something clean, but she also knew her dresser drawers would scrape if she opened them, and it wasn't like she'd spilled anything on herself at dinner.

Her backpack was partially under the bed. She pulled it out and froze. What did you put into a bag for running away? Her piggy bank was half-full, and she knew she'd need money, but it also jingled and jangled, and even padding it with the rest of her laundry wouldn't stop the coins from bouncing around. She had her twenty dollars of birthday money still on top of the dresser, and that could go in the bag. That was easy.

Her favorite doll, her stuffed monkey, they both went into the bag, and she stepped into her shoes before slinging the bag over her shoulder and carefully, carefully easing her bedroom door open and peeking into the hall. There was no sign of Tyler. She could hear the sound of the television drifting up from the downstairs living room.

Good. The one thing about this new house that was better than the old one: the floors didn't creak. They were new and level and perfect, and as long as she stayed close to the wall, she could move like a ghost, even going up and down the stairs. She walked rather than creeping, confident in her understanding of the acoustics.

The television cast flickering shadows on the walls. Antsy passed silent and swift, and thanks to the placement of the couch, neither Tyler nor her mother saw her go.

She stopped when she reached the kitchen, looking around for food she could take without opening anything, without disturbing anything. There was fruit in the big bowl by the stove, and a whole loaf of bread. The peanut butter had been left on the counter after lunch, inviting and easy to grab. She stuffed all those things into her pack, careful to stay as quiet as possible, before making her silent way to the back door.

This was it, then. She could go back to her room right now, could put her nightgown back on and pretend this had all been a dream, and call her grandparents tomorrow, to beg them to come and get her. But would they listen? If her mother told them she was just acting out, which story would they believe? Staying here wouldn't promise her safety. It would just promise she was still close enough for Tyler to get to, and she knew she wasn't safe here.

So she eased the back door open and slipped into the night, and by the time it swung shut on its own and her mother came to investigate the sound, she was long gone, out of the yard and heading down the street, backpack over her shoulder and tears running down her cheeks. She was never going back. She knew that, as completely as she knew she'd had to go, and so she just kept on going.

She kept on going all the way to the end of her street and turned, heading into unfamiliar neighborhoods, one redhaired little girl in a denim jacket and corduroy pants walking into the night, alone.

THE NEIGHBORHOOD STREETS GAVE way to a main street, busy with cars and bright with lights even after eight o'clock at night. Antsy paused, considering the wisdom of retreating back into the safer, darker residential streets, but forced herself to keep on walking. Her maternal grandparents might not believe her, but her father's mother would. She knew that. If she could find a store that would let her use their phone, she could call and ask for rescue; she could ask her grandmother to come and get her, and she knew calling from a place that wasn't home would just make her story—her *true* story—all the more believable.

The first shopping plaza she found was built around a supermarket, lights bright and artificially white. They looked too much like the lights in Target and she shied away, looking for another option. There was a liquor store, but that didn't seem like the kind of place that would want a little girl coming inside, no matter how much trouble she said she was in. There was a McDonald's, but she'd been with her mother when she got a flat tire once, and no one at the McDonald's they had gone to had been willing to let her use their phone.

And there was a little store with junk-filled windows, light seeping through the cracks between the items. Antsy drifted toward it. She hadn't realized they lived this close to a thrift store now. She loved thrift stores. They were like scavenger hunts every single time you went there, and things were usually cheap enough that when she found something really good, she could even keep it if she wanted to.

The sign on the door read ANTHONY & SONS, TRINKETS AND TREASURES. Someone had used a big black marker and written something else on the very top of the doorframe. Antsy couldn't imagine how tall that person would have needed to be.

Be sure, said the words scrawled above the door. Well, she was. She was sure it was cold out here, and the store would probably close soon, and she needed to get inside before someone saw her and asked where her parents were. She was sure she couldn't go home.

She pushed the door open and stepped through.

5 HOW TO GET LOST

THE BELL OVER THE door jingled softly as it swung closed behind her, and Antsy gazed in awestruck wonder at the shop she had stepped into. It was a glorious cacophony of things, every shelf piled high with books and antique vases and dishes and chests overflowing with jewels or coins from countries she didn't recognize or tiny, polished bones, as white as chalk. She started walking again when she noticed that the ceiling was just as crowded, dripping with stuffed birds and model airplanes. It felt like the junk shop she'd been looking for her entire life, and she couldn't decide what to look at as she walked slowly forward, looking for the counter.

A staircase up stretched along the righthand wall, books stacked on each step, so only a narrow path was left between them, and she wanted to run up those stairs, see what other treasures might be waiting for a quick, clever little girl to find. She had stopped crying, although she didn't realize it yet, and her tears were drying on her cheeks.

"Hello, young miss, and can I help you? I would ask if I *might* help you, but I know I'm allowed, this is my shop and you're clearly a patron, come through the Door just now," and the way the new voice said the word "door" was funny, placing too much importance and emphasis on it. More than it deserved. "I am absolutely *allowed* to help you, and so the question becomes whether I *can* help you, for perhaps you didn't mean to come here. Perhaps you're only passing through and not seeking for something you've lost or answering my advertisement! Perhaps there is nothing I can do for you at all."

Half of what the voice said made no sense, and the other half was too fast and hence confusing. Antsy frowned, turning toward the source of the voice.

Then she paused, even more confused, frown growing deeper and voice dying in her throat as she studied the sight in front of her. There was no one there, as she had assumed there would be; instead, an enormous bird with mostly black and white feathers, save for a blue patch at the bottom of its wings, was perching atop one of the nearest shelves. She blinked as she realized the bird was wearing a tiny pair of wire-framed glasses. It was the biggest bird she'd ever seen, bigger even than the macaw at the pet store near their old house, and they were the tiniest glasses, and that would have been funny, if it hadn't been so confusing.

Then the bird opened its beak and said, a little impatiently, "Well? *Can* I help you?"

Antsy squeaked, feeling her eyes get so wide that it hurt her face, and took two big steps backward. Not clever: that was enough to collide with the nearest shelf and send folding paper fans and tiny balsawood boxes cascading down over her. They didn't hurt, but the noise they made was immense, and somehow, that was one thing too many on top of everything else that had already happened. Antsy began to cry again, not quietly at all this time; no, she sobbed, huge braying sobs that shook her whole body and knocked more things off the shelf.

The bird looked alarmed. "Please, please, miss, stop your crying! I don't trade in the tears of children, the people who want to buy those type of things are never the sort of patrons I'm looking to attract, they bring the whole tenor of the place

down, so you're simply wasting them! Please, I'll help you if I can and if you'll let me, but I need you to *stop* crying!"

Antsy—who had run away from home and stumbled into a place where birds wore glasses and asked questions, and who had the vague feeling that on top of everything else she'd lost tonight, she had managed to lose her way—kept crying as she sank to the floor, sticking her legs straight out in front of her and slumping there like a broken doll. Her sobs gradually dwindled in power and intensity, until they were no longer shaking the shelf, and it didn't seem like there was anything else to fall on her by that point. She stayed slumped on the ground.

The bird spread its wings and hopped down from its perch, going into an easy glide that ended when its feet hit the ground and it began walking, in that jerky, head-bobbing way birds had, toward her. Antsy froze, watching it come. She had the vague feeling that she should yell or try to bat it away somehow, but she couldn't quite find the strength to move.

She had dropped her backpack when she sat down, if her graceless descent could really be called "sitting down." It was odd, and a little awkward, that the action of sitting and the process of sitting were described by the same word; it felt like there should be a difference. And she didn't know why that seemed so important when a bird was talking to her. Nothing should have been important except for the bird.

Her tears stopped, chased away by her confusion over her own priorities, and she watched the bird approach, sniffling a little. Crying was like anything else; it didn't matter whether it started all at once, it never stopped that way. Even when the tears were gone and dried and over, there was always snot.

There was probably a lesson in that, but she didn't have time to dwell on it, because the bird was close enough now to peck at her backpack, tugging at the zipper until it slid open and the bird could stick its head inside. It pulled it back out a moment later, fixing Antsy with one small, bright eye.

"You have quite a lot of food in here for someone who's just come shopping or to answer an advertisement," said the bird. "I'm not good at knowing how old humans are—you're all so unnecessarily big that it doesn't seem to matter much—but I think you're a fairly new one. Is that right?"

Antsy, who was still not sure she wanted to have an actual conversation with a bird, sniffed and nodded, staying exactly where she was.

The bird ruffled its feathers, seeming pleased to have deduced correctly. "Then I would guess, given your reaction to everything around you, that you haven't come to answer my advertisement at all, or even seen it. I would say that you were running away from your nest, and you got lost, and that's how you ended up here."

Antsy blinked, puzzling her way through all that. And then she nodded. "I ran away from home," she said. "My father . . . my father, he died, and my mother married a new, bad man, and he said if I tried to tell on him, he'd tell her I was lying, and I know she'd believe him, because she's believed him before when he told lies, and I couldn't stay there anymore. I couldn't stay or he was . . . he was going to . . ." The shape of what he'd been intending was huge and incomprehensible, veiled behind all the experiences she hadn't had yet, all the things she hadn't learned. She only knew that it was terrible and unspeakable, and something she should never have needed to fear in her own home. Something so impossibly *wrong* that even seeing it clearly might have broken her.

Antsy burst into tears again. The bird danced backward, wings half-spread, and squawked an alarmed, "No, no, human, no, don't cry! Oh, please don't cry. Please don't— Vineta! Vineta, I need you!" The bird launched itself into the air, still calling for someone named Vineta, which was a name Antsy had never heard before.

She kept crying. Crying was something she could understand, and there were so few things she could understand right now that holding on to the one she *did* have made all the rest seem like less of a loss. She tugged her backpack closer to herself, protecting its precious cargo of sandwiches-yet-to-be. She hadn't taken a bread knife and wasn't sure how she was supposed to *make* sandwiches, but she'd figure it out soon enough, just as soon as she got out of here and back to somewhere where the birds didn't try to carry on conversations with her.

She might have enjoyed it on any other night, or if her mother had been here with her, or if things had been different in any possible way. A talking bird was magical and strange, and strange, magical things were delightful, but not when the world already felt like it had been flipped upside down and vigorously shaken. She was off-balance and out of sorts, and she wasn't in the mood for magic.

The bird came swooping back to its original perch, folding its wings as it landed and looking down at her for a few seconds before calling, "Here! Here! Over here!"

"I'm coming, you impatient avian, I'm coming," said a cross voice. Antsy looked up in frozen terror at the sound of footsteps on the floor, and then an old woman, old as anything, probably older than *everything,* came creaking around the edge of the shelves. She had white hair piled high atop her head and secured with half a dozen long wooden and ivory hair sticks, and seamed golden-brown skin so serrated with wrinkles that her face was like a photograph of a maze, taken from high above the ground. Her eyes, though, were black and bright and very sharp, and they twinkled in the light as she peered down at the huddling Antsy.

She was wearing a long blue bathrobe embroidered with row upon row of peach blossoms, the pattern picked out in gold and pink thread, the occasional fat, round fruit peeking out from between the petals.

"Hello, girl," said the woman, and stooped, one hand remaining on her heavy walking stick, her knuckles so large and gnarled that they looked almost like peach pits themselves. "Where have you come from?"

Antsy sniffled and shrank away, but she had been raised to be polite to people older than she was, and this woman qualified if anyone ever had, or ever would again. "The parking lot, ma'am," she said.

"She speaks the common tongue," said the woman to the bird. "So she's lost, but not so lost as all of that. She's not come from my namesake, if that was your concern. Sell her a bit of frippery and send her on her way, and we'll sit down to supper as we should have already done."

Antsy stared at the woman for what must have been a beat too long, because she frowned, eyes still on Antsy.

"Well?" she asked. "Where did you lose your way?"

"I . . . I didn't," said Antsy. "I didn't lose it at all. I know right where I am."

The woman chuckled, low and dark. "I sincerely doubt that, child."

"I do! I went out the back door and I walked all the way along the street until it met the big street we drive on every morning to take me to school, and then I turned left and I was in the parking lot where the grocery store is." Antsy sat up straighter, annoyed by the very idea that she could be lost. "Your light was on. So I came to the door, to see if anyone here could help me. I need to find a phone so I can call my grandmother and tell her I had to run away."

"You ran away?" When Antsy nodded, the woman did the same, looking pleased with herself.

"There, she's lost enough to find her way here," said the woman. "I'm afraid, child, that you've gone considerably farther from home than you meant to. When you found the door that brought you to us, was there anything written on it?"

"It said *Anthony & Sons, Trinkets and Treasures*," said Antsy. She paused, then asked, "Are you Anthony?" It could be a last name, she supposed, like hers was Ricci, or her mother's was Richards now that she was married to Tyler. He'd wanted Antsy to take his last name too, and she'd refused, saying she liked the name she had, and so they'd stapled his name onto hers like an extra piece of paper.

"No, child, I'm not," said the woman. Then she cocked her head, and said, in a wondering tone, "Anthony and Sons? That's what the door says when it goes fishing on . . . Were there any other words, child? Any other words at all? They may not have been on the door itself. They could have been written on the sidewalk, or on a window, or anywhere that you'd be able to see them."

Antsy bit her lip. "Yes," she said, after a moment. "Someone wrote on the doorframe. It wasn't me. I'm not tall enough, and it wasn't a right thing to do."

"What did they write?" prompted the woman.

"*Be sure*," said Antsy.

The woman straightened up, clinging to her cane for balance. "There, you stupid bird," she said smugly. "She's ours, and it doesn't matter if she saw the advertisement or not, because she's been put here, right and proper, and we'll see to her or we'll answer the reasons why before a council of our betters."

"I'm not *yours*," protested Antsy, grabbing her backpack and getting indignantly to her feet. The urge to stomp and shout was strong, but that was how *little* kids handled their problems, and she wasn't a little kid at all, so she just glared. "I'm not *anyone's*. I didn't mean to bother anyone, and I'm sorry I knocked your things down, but I'm not here to answer any advertisem . . . adverti . . . anything! I'm here because the light was on and I wanted to use the phone!"

"Earth," said the woman to the bird, as if this explained everything. The bird made a croaking noise, and Antsy's anger got even bigger, burning in her chest like a candle. Candles start with small flames, but they can become house fires quickly enough if not watched carefully. "America, too, by the sound of her. They still think they're the only place there is."

"You don't get to own me because I bumped a shelf," said Antsy.

"We don't own you, child—and what's your name, anyway? I can't keep calling you 'child' forever. For one thing, it won't always be true, and for another thing, it's not very kind. People should be themselves, not just part of a classification. For example, my name is Vineta, and this pompous old fellow is my colleague, Hudson."

The bird puffed out the feathers on his chest before bobbing his head at Antsy and saying, brightly, "It's nice to meet you."

"My name is Antsy," said Antsy.

"Short for something, or were you a very squirmy baby?"

"Antoinette."

"That's a better size name for a girl as tall as you are," said the woman.

Antsy, who had never considered herself particularly tall, blinked at her. "I would like to leave now," she said.

"If you can find the door you came in through, of course, you can leave any time you like," said the woman. "But whatever door you find, be sure you look at it carefully, and don't just go charging through. You may not like what you find waiting on the other side." There was a hungry glint in her eyes as she spoke.

Antsy nodded, doing her best to make the gesture respectful. Then she inched around the woman, keeping her back to the shelves so she never took her eyes off the woman even once, and bolted back along the way she had come. The long aisle formed by the close-set shelves was exactly as it had been when she walked along it the first time; she hadn't even knocked anything over. And there, at the end of the aisle, was the door. Antsy ran toward it as fast as she could.

But there was no wall. Antsy slowed as she realized what was missing, a slow frown growing on her face. There was no wall and there was no window, there was just a door and the frame that held it, standing in the aisle with nothing to support it.

She slowed further, until she was walking slowly, and frowned at the door as she approached. It was painted white, with two keyholes below the knob, one huge and old-fashioned, like something out of a storybook, the other just like the one on their door at home, simple, sleek, and modern. There was nothing written on the door itself.

She peeked around it. The aisle extended on the other side of the door, simple and unbroken. She returned to looking at the door itself, still frowning.

The door remained a door, unbothered by her contemplations, identical on both sides. Finally, unable to bear the silence any longer, Antsy grasped the doorknob, turned, and pulled. There was a moment of resistance, the door seeming to sense her reluctance. She pulled harder, whispering, "I'm sure," under her breath. With a creak of its hinges that sounded almost like a sigh, the door came unstuck and swung wide, a crackle like ozone hanging in the air. Antsy felt better almost instantly, her eyes no longer aching from all the crying she'd been doing, and she was suddenly too preoccupied with staring to cry.

On the other side of the door, where the shop should have been, a jungle stretched all the way to the horizon, fat, round-trunked trees dripping with vines and flowers, their twisting branches reaching for the sky like the spread fingers of enormous hands. Something moved in the deep foliage, and brightly colored birds perched on the vines, clacking their beaks and calling to each other at the sight of her.

It wasn't possible. It wasn't logical. It wasn't *real*. It couldn't be real.

Antsy stepped through the door. Only one foot; she was at least clever enough to leave her other foot solidly on the wooden floor of the thrift store. One of the vast, bright-petaled flowers was close enough for her to lean over and pluck it before retreating back through the door and closing it behind her. The flower didn't disintegrate when pulled into the thrift store. It remained in her hand, bright and blooming, petals almost the same color as a good, ripe watermelon.

She stared at it, trying to understand how this could be happening. Something clattered behind her. She turned, and there was Hudson, perching atop another shelf, watching her.

"Not what you expected?" he asked. "Or not what you wanted?"

"I didn't— I wasn't— I couldn't— This isn't real! Doors

lead into rooms, not *jungles!*" She brandished the flower at him like he would somehow understand how wrong this all was simply because a flower that looked like watermelon but smelled like cherries was in his face.

Hudson looked at the flower critically. "Smells good," he said. "Could have made nice tea. I wish you'd kept that Door open longer, Vineta might have been able to harvest something we could sell. Oh, well. Suppose it can't be helped now." He took the flower's stem daintily in his beak and jumped into the air, wings beating hard as he turned and flew back toward the old woman.

Antsy stared after him. Her eyes were starting to hurt from all the staring she'd been doing. The smell of the flower still hung in the air, luscious and inviting. She hadn't meant for Hudson to take it away from her the way he had. She'd been intending to keep it for a little while, as a reminder of how ridiculous this whole night was.

She frowned, and kept frowning as she turned back to the door. One more flower couldn't hurt anything . . .

The door stuck again, resisting her until she really *committed* to pulling on the knob, and when it finally did swing open, it was on something completely different, entirely new, although there was again the smell of ozone, again the feeling of serenity. There was no jungle. There was no parking lot, either. Instead, a vast outdoor market stretched in front of her, stalls packed tight together and teeming with people. At least she thought they were people. She'd never seen people with fur before, or people colored blue and purple, a whole spectrum of those two colors. They had ears and tails like cats, but they wore long robes patterned in triangles and sharp lines to contrast with the rosettes on their bodies.

As she watched, a child ran up to one of the larger cat-people, a bundle of what looked like electric pink grapes in its hand-paws. It offered the "grapes" to the adult, who plucked one and ate it before patting the child indulgently on the head.

Antsy began to swing the door shut. A hand from behind her stopped it, and she looked over her shoulder to see Vineta standing there. "No, not right away," she said. "It's been some time since we've seen a proper market, and I could use a great deal of fruit. Hudson! Do you recognize this one?"

"Mmmm . . . Dejaniran, I'd say, from the shape of them," said Hudson. "Generally safe for women and children, not a good idea for me. They're hunters, and I'm likely to suit their idea of prey."

"Then it's your turn to watch the door. Wait here, Antoinette. Don't live up to your nickname just yet." Vineta vanished into the rows of shelves. Antsy could tell her general location from the sound of rattling and rustling, right up until Vineta popped back into view, now carrying two large wicker baskets. She offered one to Antsy, who hesitated before taking it, not seeing any way out of the situation that didn't involve running screaming into the impossible market.

"Good girl," said Vineta approvingly. "Now, a few ground rules: if this isn't Dejanira, it's close enough to Dejanira that the people are probably very *like* the Dejaniran, meaning you mustn't run or move too quickly, ever. Movement attracts and excites them, and the young ones especially are inclined to pounce on anything that catches their eyes. The older ones will have learned better manners, but they'll still be interested if you move too quickly, and we're about to be uninvited guests. Do you understand?"

"Not even a little bit," said Antsy.

That appeared to be the correct answer, because Vineta nodded and handed her an envelope filled with coins that clanked against each other in unfamiliar ways. The weight of them was satisfying, even if she couldn't possibly have guessed how much money she now held.

"We're going shopping," said Vineta. "I know what we need; your job is finding what we don't know we need yet, since you'll have no preconceptions about what can be bought at a market like this one."

Antsy blinked slowly. "What do you mean?"

"I mean if something catches your eye, buy it and put it in your basket, and when your basket is full, return to the Door. Hudson will make sure it doesn't close. Nothing alive, please, sometimes those don't handle the transition well, as you clearly haven't. Now come along, we have no idea what the market hours are." Vineta stepped through the door and started toward the first rank of stalls, not looking back to verify that Antsy was following.

Antsy didn't *want* to follow a woman she'd only just met through a mysterious door and into a market filled with cat-people who might chase her if she got excited and moved too fast, both things she was profoundly inclined to do. She also didn't want to stay behind, alone, with a talking bird when she'd only have to deal with Vineta upon the woman's return. She stepped cautiously through the doorway.

Putting her first foot through felt the same way it had in the jungle, like she was just taking a step. Putting her second foot through was harder, like she was trying to drag her body through the thickest soap bubble she had ever encountered. But after only a few seconds, she was through, and when she looked back, the open door was still there, with the shop behind it, just . . . faded somehow, made faint and unobtrusive. Cat-people should have been staring at it, thronging for this impossible thing that had opened in their midst, and instead they were going about their business, ignoring it completely.

Vineta was already gone, swallowed by the crowd, which seemed less like a movie and more like a real thing now that Antsy was actually a part of it. The people had a smell. Not an unpleasant one, but a smell like a cat that had been out in the afternoon sun for hours, baking sunlight into its fur. They smelled hot and vital and alive and *real*. They weren't the only smell in the air, either. A cacophony of fruits and flowers tickled her nose, and under them was the sweet, almost-familiar scent of baking bread.

Her mouth watered and her stomach grumbled, and she turned, almost without intending it, to follow the smell of baking deeper into the maze of stalls.

She looked nothing like the cat-people around her, but none of them stopped her or even looked at her twice. She passed stalls selling fruit she'd never seen before; stalls selling nuts roasted and poured into twists of paper; stalls selling flowers and jams and jellies and what looked like jars of golden honey. Everywhere she looked, there was something new to see.

Despite the impossible crowd, she caught several glimpses of Vineta, who didn't seem to be following her, only making her own way through the market; Vineta's attention was on the merchants who took her strange copper coins in exchange for the items she placed in her basket. Antsy kept walking, and felt better when Vineta didn't follow. The idea of an adult following her right now was . . .

It wasn't good. She might never know exactly what Tyler had intended, but she knew she had been lucky to escape it, and she knew she didn't ever want to be in that position again, not even with a little old lady who looked like a stiff wind might knock her over. Antsy kept following the scent in the air.

Then she came around a corner, and there was the stall. It was being operated by a bright blue cat-person with paler blue rosettes on their cheeks, wearing another of those long robes, and the counter was covered in an assortment of baked goods that would have put every bakery she'd ever passed to shame. There were croissants and danishes, and folded pastries she didn't know the names for but that she longed to taste. Her stomach growled. Antsy drifted closer, until the merchant took notice.

"A traveler child," the merchant said, sounding surprised but not displeased. His words were a little oddly shaped, accented by the shape of his muzzle, but they were comprehensible all the same. Antsy met his eyes and froze, not sure what to do.

The merchant blinked, whiskers shifting forward in a way that meant friendliness and curiosity from a smaller cat. "To here, or to somewhere close on here? We don't often see furless travelers in the market. You tend to be uncomfortable and can't read us half the time, and so it seems likely you might be from somewhere close."

"I, um," said Antsy. Then, with an air of desperation, "I have money. I'm supposed to buy whatever interests me and put it in my basket and then go back to the door. Hudson's keeping it open so we can go back when we're done with the shopping. He didn't come shopping because he's a bird."

"Yes, this is not a good place for birds," said the merchant. "I'll make you a bargain, traveler child: reach into whatever purse you have, and give me the first thing your fingers touch.

I'll give you twice its value in pastry, as a gift of welcome, *and* I'll tell you which way you should go next, if you're meant to buy whatever interests you."

"*Everything* is interesting here," said Antsy, a little plaintively. But it was true. This place was so new, so unfamiliar, and so brightly colored, it felt like she'd been dropped in the middle of a parade on television, or in an amusement park the way they looked in the commercials, where there were no lines and no sunburns and princesses appeared with open arms every time you went around a corner. It was all so much.

"Yes, but a thing being interesting doesn't mean it has to interest *you*," said the merchant. "That's what a market test is, for you travelers; it's to see if you have good instincts when it comes to what catches your eye. And so far, I'd say you're passing. I make the best pastries in this whole market. Not the cheapest, but I have the finest butter and the hottest oven, and what I lack in affordability, I balance out with quality."

For the first time, Antsy looked alarmed. "What if the first thing my fingers touch isn't even worth a roll?"

"Then I'll give you whatever you ask for anyway, as welcome and well-met." The merchant's whiskers pushed forward again. Oh, that had to be a smile. There was no other way to explain it. Antsy smiled back, careful not to show her teeth. She remembered dogs didn't like it when people showed their teeth, and maybe cats were the same way.

She reached into the envelope she'd been given, brushing her fingers against the top of what felt like a solid wall of coins. Then she grasped the first one that distinguished itself from the rest and pulled it out, revealing a flat silvery disc about the size of a half-dollar, with a stern-looking cat-person in three-quarters profile and tiny, unfamiliar writing all around the edges. She held it solemnly out toward the merchant, whose eyes widened.

"I did not offer you a kindly bargain to cheat you," he said, in a strangled voice.

Antsy frowned, glancing to the coin in her palm and then back up again. "Is this not enough?" she asked.

"Child, that is . . . that is a silver phoenix, from the reign of our first Empress. It's worth more than my entire stall put together."

"But we made a deal," said Antsy. "And when Vineta gave me this money, she did it expecting me to spend it. Can we make another deal?"

"What deal would that be?" asked the merchant, eyes still on the coin.

"I give you the coin, and you let me have whatever I want from the things you're selling, then you give the rest away to whoever wants it, and you come show me around the market for a little while. I'll be able to relax and look at things more if I'm not afraid of getting lost, and you can tell me if I'm trying to pay someone who's not as honest as you are more than I should."

The merchant, who clearly wanted the coin, blinked at her. Then he laughed, delighted. "So we both get the better of the deal," he said. "You get sweets for later, I look like a generous soul, and you have a guide for the day, while I make my week's profits in a moment. If you would not feel ill-done by, I would be glad to take your offered bargain." He held his hand out, waiting for the coin.

Antsy smiled and dropped it into his purple-leathered palm, watching as he made it disappear. Then he spread his hands to indicate the wealth of delicacies in front of him. "Now, traveler child, what does your heart desire?"

In that moment, in a strange market on a different world, contemplating an assortment of treats she'd never tasted before, about to be escorted through a market by a talking cat-person, Antsy's heart desired nothing more than to stay here forever, and to never, never, ever go home.

In that moment, she was finally sure.

6 AFTER THE MARKET

WHEN ANTSY RETURNED TO the door, her new friend in tow—his name was Sákos, and he had been selling his baking at the market for fifteen years, and this was the first time anyone had ever purchased the bulk of his wares with the intention of giving them away—the basket Vineta had given her was packed to overflowing with every little thing that had managed to catch her eye, pastries and breads and jams and honeys and several kinds of unfamiliar fruit and even a bag of roast nuts that she thought Hudson might enjoy. She had a vague idea that birds liked to eat seeds, and nuts were a kind of seed, weren't they?

Sákos carried a second basket, even larger than the first, and equally filled with treasures from the market. Most of Antsy's coins had proven to be antiques on a level with the first, and even the smallest purchase had left the merchants unsure of how they could possibly give her change. Several more vendors had found themselves in the enviable position of having sold their entire stock to someone who, after taking what she wanted, was more than happy to walk away from the rest, leaving it to be given out freely or sold a second time, as the merchants saw fit.

It had taken less than fifteen minutes for Sákos to distribute the items Antsy didn't take from his stall. As soon as the market children had realized he wasn't playing a cruel joke when he announced everything he had was free for the rest of the day, they had swarmed like so many fluffy piranha, and while there had been some squabbling over particularly desirable treats—all things Sákos had been careful to point out to Antsy before he began calling anyone over, allowing her to have the best of the lot—in the end, every child who came within range of the stall walked away with something to enjoy. A few of them cast curious glances at Antsy as they trotted back to their parents with hands full of treats, trying to figure out the strange, furless figure with the overflowing basket of goodies, but none of them questioned her, and in the end, Sákos had been free to escort her around the rest of the place.

It had been, in all, one of the best days Antsy could remember. Everyone had been excruciatingly pleasant once they realized she was with Sákos and, more, that she had coin to spend. And that had been before they realized the value of the coin. Not all of them were quite as honest as he was, and from the way their whiskers flattened when they saw that her guide was going to make sure she was treated well, she guessed some of them would have enjoyed the chance to cheat her.

But now, both her baskets were full, and her feet hurt. They approached the pale, wavering outline of the door. Vineta was already there, waiting, her own basket still singular but equally full, although her purchases also featured several bottles of wine and oil, and she had bundles of flowers dangling from the belt of her robe. She smiled when she saw Antsy and Sákos approach, and if there was a sliver of relief in that expression, it wasn't as important as the pleasure in her eyes.

"I see you found a friend," she said, gaze flicking to Sákos. "How did this happen?"

"Are you this child's guardian?" asked Sákos.

"Guardian, no. Companion, yes, at least for now. She came

through into the shop where I serve, and this is her testing ground. Did she do well?"

"She offered me a silver phoenix from the reign of the first Empress for a *roll*."

Vineta looked politely puzzled. "Was that not enough?"

"It was enough to buy my wares for the day, and for the rest of the sennight if she had wished to claim them also," he said. "You did the girl no favors by letting her loose on her own, with no idea what she was walking into and such a purse."

"It seems I did her plenty of favors, as it brought her to you," said Vineta. "The test is twofold. Can the new applicants navigate the space, and can they trust their own instincts? From what she carries, I would say she has no trouble in that department, and from your presence, I can further intuit that she took no time in trusting her instincts. I thank you for assisting her, and we'll be going now."

"Going? Going where?"

"Back to the place where we began." Vineta looked to Antsy. "Get your things and thank the man, and we'll be on our way."

Antsy knew an order when she heard one. She reached her free hand out for the basket Sákos carried, and when he handed it to her, she smiled. "Thank you for helping me," she said.

"No, thank *you* for paying me enough that my family will eat very well for the next few weeks," he said. "Will we see you here again?"

"It's always possible, if the Doors will it," said Vineta. "Come, Antsy."

She turned then and stepped through the hazy doorway,

disappearing. Sákos shook his head. "I've seen travelers come and go before, but it never ceases to be amazing, how you vanish into empty air," he said.

Antsy blinked. It wasn't empty air. The door was *right there*. How was it he didn't seem to see it? "Thank you again," she said. "It was very nice to meet you."

"And you as well, child," he said, whiskers pushed forward. "If you come this way again, seek me. You will always have food at my table, and when you tire of tolls and time, we would welcome you well."

That seemed to be as good a goodbye as she was going to get, and so Antsy turned, staggering a little under the weight of her baskets, and stepped through the door. As she had only half-expected, she found herself in the store, Hudson peering at her from his perch atop the nearest shelf.

Vineta stooped, removing a rock that someone—it couldn't have been Hudson, he was a bird, and birds didn't have hands—had wedged between the door and frame to keep it from closing. When she straightened, the door swung shut with a decisive click, and Antsy felt an odd, distant pang of loss, like something had just gone away for a long time, if not forever.

"Well, we're all here, so let's see what we have," said Vineta, and began walking away. Hudson swooped after her, and Antsy brought up the rear, staggering under the weight of her two baskets.

With Vineta in the lead, they quickly found the counter that had eluded Antsy before. It was a vast barrier of a thing, old, scarred wood worn smooth by an uncounted number of hands, half-shielded by a leather blotter. The register was ancient, antique and slightly rusty, and next to it, a hardwood perch had been bolted to the counter itself. Hudson alighted on that perch, preening his wings with his beak and looking pleased with himself.

"Come on, you stupid bird," said Vineta mildly, and kept walking, through a little swinging door that read *Employees Only* in fancy gothic script. She looked back once she was on the other side, raising an eyebrow at Antsy. "Well?" she asked. "Are you coming?"

Antsy wasn't entirely sure she wanted to. Passing through that little swinging door felt like it would be making a promise, somehow, like she would be committing herself to something she couldn't understand or take back. But Vineta was waiting for her, and these baskets were heavy, and she couldn't wait here forever. She had to make a choice.

She chose to keep moving. The swinging door swung shut again behind her, and Hudson jumped into the air, smoothly gliding over to land on Vineta's shoulder, and together the three of them made their way past shelves crowded with incoming and returned merchandise, into the depths of the shop.

A BEADED CURTAIN SEPARATED the employee break room from the hall that ran the length of the rest of the private spaces, thick and golden and weirdly effective at blocking them from view. There was a circular table at the center of the room, which otherwise held a few chairs, a shelf of dry goods, and something that looked for all the world like a wind-up refrigerator.

Vineta set her basket on the table, following it with the bundles of flowers from her belt, and handed the envelope with her remaining money to Hudson, who took it delicately in his beak and cocked his head, as solemn as if he was weighing out its contents. Finally, sounding pleased, he transferred

the envelope to one claw and said, "More than half left. If we find it again, you'll have a sense of going prices." Then he jumped into the air again and flew over to the shelf, dropping the envelope at the very top and swooping back to land on the basket's handle and look expectantly at Antsy.

"Hudson does our accounting," said Vineta. "Magpies aren't the best corvids when it comes to counting your coins, but they do well enough."

"Hush," said Hudson. "The rhyme was about us first and the crows stole it, as you very well know. We're the best there is when it comes to keeping the books accurate and the budget balanced." He looked at Antsy again, finally prompting, "Well? Did you spend it *all*?"

"Oh—no! I'm sorry. I didn't think . . . I'm sorry." Antsy put down her baskets and pulled the envelope out of the pocket where she'd shoved it for safekeeping, offering it to Hudson. He took it delicately in his beak, repeating the process of weighing it out.

When he transferred it to his claw, it was so he could look at Antsy with new respect. "Even *more* left. You're a natural bargain-hunter, aren't you?" Then he was flying the envelope back to the shelf to join the other, while Antsy boosted her baskets onto the table and tried to decide whether she was flattered or embarrassed by what had certainly felt like it was intended to be praise.

Vineta looked at the baskets with a measuring eye. "You're sure you didn't steal anything?" she asked. "I won't be angry if you did, but it's best if we can keep a record of which markets may not be happy to see us again."

"What? No!" said Antsy, stung. "Sákos made sure no one cheated me, or charged me too much because they could tell I didn't know what I was spending, and I trust him to have been true about it because he could have taken everything I had for just one cookie if he'd wanted to, back when I was trying to buy from him. He was very good to me. Everyone at the market was kind."

"Children often inspire that response in adults, even when they aren't the same species," said Vineta. "How old are you, girl?"

Antsy wanted to be taken seriously, and she thought Vineta might be so old that she didn't have any idea how old children were anymore. They were younger than her, but so was everyone else in the world. So she stood up straighter, and took a deep breath to make herself seem taller and thicker in the middle, and said, "Nine."

"Nine's a fine age," said Vineta. "You're a small nine, too, which will help. Hopefully it lasts and we can get some good years off you before you're on stock duty."

Antsy blinked. "Stock duty? Years?"

"Small children are good at working the Doors. That one you found doesn't open for me anymore at all, hasn't in years, and neither will any of the others, but they know you well enough to let you through," said Vineta. She turned her eyes to the baskets and began sorting through them as she spoke, lifting items out one by one and placing them on the table. "That will start to fade eventually. It fades for everyone, and that's a good warning to have, because there's a point past which it won't be safe for you to go through any Door you open for yourself. Once someone else has opened a Door, you know where it goes, and you can come and go as you please, as you feel the need."

Antsy's head was starting to spin. "That's not how doors work," she protested.

Vineta paused, a jar of sunshine-yellow jam in one hand,

and looked curiously at Antsy. "Really? You're an expert on Doors, then, you know everything about them? So tell me, expert, how *do* Doors work? Because we've wanted to know that for years and years. How they work, and how they pick the people they're going to steal away, and more, how they decide where they're going to send them. Why, if we could use even one Door reliably, we could be richer than all the empires in the history of all the worlds there are."

Antsy blinked slowly. "Doors open in one place and when you go through, you're in another place. Like the door of my bedroom opens on the hallway, and when I go through, I'm either in the hallway or my bedroom. No other places."

"She doesn't know what's happened," said Hudson. "Think way, way back, before the continents shifted in their positions. You didn't always know, either. Your first Door was a surprise to you."

"It was certainly *something*," said Vineta. "I just wish it had been a surprise a little sooner than it was. I was fifteen and running from the marriage my parents had negotiated for me, and I got less than a year before the Doors stopped working when I tried to open them. What I wouldn't give to have been *nine*. You have such adventures ahead of you, child."

"Years?" said Antsy again.

Vineta sighed. She put down the cluster of pink grapes she'd been holding and turned fully to Antsy, expression grave. "I'm going to make some guesses," she said. "You seem clean and well fed and healthy, so you didn't run away a long time ago. Someone loves you. Someone has been taking care of you. And then something bad happened. Something bad enough that you looked at all that love and all that care and decided that they weren't enough to balance out the size of the bad thing. Am I close?"

Antsy bit her lip and nodded.

"All right. So you ran away from home, and you were very, very sure you were doing the right thing, that the world would be better somehow if you could just get lost and disappear like a snowflake in a storm. And then you found a door that said to be sure, and you *were* sure, you were already sure, you were so sure that when you tried the knob, it wasn't locked, and you could walk right through."

She paused then, creating a silence that lingered until Antsy filled it with a whispered "My mother believed him because he was better than me, and believing me would have been believing a bad girl who told bad lies about good people."

"I don't think that's true, Antsy," said Vineta. "You're a child. If an adult hurt you, that's on them, not on you. Being bruised doesn't make you bad, unless you're a peach, and even a bruised peach is good for making jam."

Antsy looked at her with narrowed eyes but couldn't see any sign that she was lying, and felt a small knot that had formed inside her heart loosen and let go. Suddenly she could almost breathe again.

Vineta returned to unpacking the baskets. "Whatever bad thing this person did or was getting ready to do, it was bad enough you needed to get away from there. Maybe running away wasn't the best choice you could have made, but it was the choice you chose, and the Doors respected it. I wish you were an expert, though."

"She's certainly a good bargainer," said Hudson, head cocked, studying a slice of some sort of delicately scented fruit cake with one small black eye. "I've never seen anyone bring back so much on their first visit."

"That's true," said Vineta. "I told you to buy whatever

caught your interest. What made these things catch your interest?"

"The muffins and cookies and things smelled good," said Antsy, haltingly. "And after that, I just bought whatever seemed pretty, or interesting, or not like anything at the stalls around it. The second basket was because there was so much market, and I'd gotten so much baked stuff that the first basket was almost all the way filled before we could even get started."

"Children get bargains the rest of us can't," said Vineta. She sat down in one of the chairs, a fruit that looked like a turquoise mango in one hand. Producing a small pocketknife from inside her robe, she began to peel it.

"As you've probably managed to guess, Antsy, this is a junk shop," she said. "We sell lost things here, and anything that's lost winds up here, in our storeroom or the attic. We sort through it, we price it, and we shelve it, and then it sits until someone comes looking for it. On the rare occasions when one of the original owners shows up, we return their property, no questions asked, although if it's sold before they come looking, there's nothing to be done for them. And when a Door appears, if we have someone on staff who can open it, we go through and we go shopping."

"How did you get all that money?"

"People lose money all the time," said Hudson. "And money is interesting because it gets less valuable as it remains in circulation, but more valuable after it's fallen out of circulation."

Antsy looked confused.

Vineta flicked a bit of mango peel at Hudson. "She's a *child*, birdbrain, don't ask her to understand things she has no reason to know about yet! All the Doors connect places where there are people, and people are essentially the same everywhere that we can go. They can look very, very different, like Hudson here doesn't look like you, and you don't look like me, but they're still people, and being people means they're going to approach some things in similar ways. The Doors don't tend to open on worlds where people eat children who aren't related to them, for example."

"Do worlds like that exist?" asked Antsy, horrified.

Vineta nodded. "They do, and we've had people from them pass through, when *they* ran away from something bad that was trying very hard to happen to them. But we've never seen a Door from here to there, and I've never heard of someone who ran away like that going back."

"One of them did," said Hudson. "Once he was old enough that he wasn't at risk of the dinner table any longer, he opened a closet and there was his home on the other side, waiting for him like nothing had changed. And he looked so *happy*, I guess that was where he belonged after all. He was only sure he didn't want to be eaten, not that eating people was a bad thing."

Antsy didn't like the sound of that. She pulled a sour face. "I don't want to go anywhere like *that*," she said. "But how do I go home?"

"Is that really what you want?" asked Vineta. "You ran away. Whatever you were running from, it's still going to be there, and you were sure you needed to escape. Has something changed that makes you think you wouldn't be in danger anymore if you went back?"

Antsy bit her lip and shook her head. She didn't have the vocabulary to explain that what had changed was her memory of the moment, panic and certainty fading into misty remove with surprising speed. The mind is bad at holding on to terror, and while she knew she'd needed to run, she was no longer as afraid, or as confident that if she went back, Tyler would try again. Maybe he wouldn't. Or maybe her mother would believe her after all. Now that she had a little distance and a little clarity, and a whole afternoon spent at an impossible market whirling in her head, she could see the flaws in Tyler's logic.

Yes, her mother had believed him about things like touching plates or losing the remote control—all small, reasonable things for her to have done, and unreasonable things for him to have lied about. But "Tyler came into my room and touched me and I didn't like it and I don't want him to do it again" wasn't a small thing, or a reasonable one. It was the sort of thing that could make her normally calm mother lose her cool completely.

She just had to be in a position to say it.

Vineta watched Antsy's face as she puzzled through her own feelings, and finally she sighed. "Well, that's as it may be, but even if you don't want anything in this moment more than you want to leave us, you can't."

"I can't?"

"I'm too old for the Doors, or too settled; they leave you alone once your roots dig deep enough, as if they can tell when you're not meant to be a traveler any longer. It's not just adulthood, although we think adulthood plays a role in things—adults tend to be more set in their ways, and more inclined to think before they take big risks—but stability. You, on the other hand . . . the Doors know you, Antoinette called Antsy. They know you, and they wanted you, or they would never have come for you in the first place."

Antsy, who wasn't sure how she felt about the idea of doors

being able to want things or decide things, blinked slowly at her. "Why does that mean I can't leave?"

"Because the Doors won't open on the world you want unless they've decided to be done with you." Vineta's smile was almost sympathetic. "It's all right. You're safe here until that happens."

Antsy bit her lip, eyes going wide and slowly horrified. Then she wailed, "But I don't even know where here *is*!"

"This is the Shop Where the Lost Things Go," said Vineta. She pronounced each word with a careful precision that made it clear she was saying the name of a thing and not just a sentence. "There's a whole world outside, filled with lost things, and now it's also filled with you."

"And you both came through doors like I did?"

"Not me," said Hudson, puffing out his chest proudly. "This is where magpies come from."

"All magpies," said Vineta. "They have magpies in almost every world where there are birds, because the doors open here so often, and sometimes magpies fly through them and don't make it back before the doors swing shut again."

"But . . . magpies don't talk," said Antsy, who felt sure she'd seen pictures of them in storybooks, and would have heard if they could carry on a conversation.

"The ones who fly through do," said Hudson. "But their babies don't, and they never remember how much they've lost by going from the Land of Lost Things to the Land of Found Things. It's a terrible thing, to be found." And he shivered, feathers puffing out until he looked like a round ball of a bird.

Antsy had a hundred more questions, but it had been hours since her bedtime, and her head was beginning to spin. So she seized on the one thing she was sure she *did* understand, and said plaintively, "You mean I really can't go home?"

"Not unless you're Found, child," said Vineta, more gently than she'd said most of her other terrible, perplexing things. "This is your home until that happens, unless you want to go through one of the doors and stay on the other side. You could, if you liked. Many people have found homes in worlds very far from the ones where they began."

Antsy wanted to argue, but not as much as she wanted to sleep. She yawned, trying hard to smother it behind her hand, and jumped as Hudson flapped over and landed on her shoulder.

"Travel can be hard," he said. "It wears on the heart, even when it's done on purpose, and there's always a cost and a consequence. Come on. I'll show you where you can sleep."

Antsy wanted so badly to argue, but she wanted even more to rest, and so she merely nodded and followed the black-and-white bird as he pushed himself back into the air and went gliding into the hall.

The employees-only portion of the Shop Where the Lost Things Go was a labyrinth, beginning with a short hall leading to four different doors. Hudson swooped so that the tip of his right wing brushed against one of them. "Here," he said. "Go here."

Obedient and exhausted, Antsy opened the door, which behaved like any other door, offering no resistance, no smell of ozone. On the other side, a flight of stairs beckoned, narrow and plain and simple. The steps were worn, unpainted wood, and the bannister was polished by the passage of many hands. Hudson swept upward, and Antsy followed to the landing, where another hallway opened out.

"This way," called the bird, and she continued following, too tired to argue.

At the end of the hall was a door.

On the other side of the door was a room. It was small, and as simple as the stairs, with white walls, a tiny dresser, and a single bed pushed up against one wall. There was a window, but it showed nothing, only the deep darkness of a lingering night. A basin of water sat atop the dresser, and Antsy's mouth was suddenly dry. "Is there a cup?" she asked. "Or a toilet?"

"Bathroom's across the hall," said Hudson. "Shop invited you in, so everything you need will be there. We'll see you when you wake up."

And he flew away, and Antsy was alone.

Cautious now, she left the room and crossed the hall. The bathroom was not as old-fashioned as she had briefly feared: there was a toilet, and a sink, and a shower, which she wrinkled her nose at and ignored. On the edge of the sink was a toothbrush, and a boar-bristle brush like the one she had at home, and a wooden hair pick and a bottle of oil like her mother used when she had to brush Antsy's hair, which would break and snarl if brushed when it was dry, and had snapped three plastic brushes in half before her mom realized those wouldn't work. Antsy ignored the hair supplies and picked up the toothbrush.

There was a tube of paste on the small shelf above the toilet when she looked around for it. She felt sure that hadn't been there a moment before; maybe Hudson was right about the shop itself making arrangements for her. After a day of talking birds and impossible doors, that wouldn't be the strangest thing ever.

Antsy brushed her teeth dutifully, used the facilities, and returned to the room where she was going to sleep. There was a nightgown folded on the pillow. Like all the linens, it smelled of lavender. She slipped it gratefully on and slid into the bed, and was asleep almost as soon as she closed her eyes.

She could figure out how to get home when she woke up. She wasn't going to do anyone any good by forcing herself to stay awake when she was already this exhausted.

And so the world slipped away into dazzling, dizzying dreams of marketplaces filled with cat-people and birds that talked, and Antsy was at peace.

PART III

STAYING LOST

7 ONE'S FOR SORROW, TWO'S FOR JOY

ANTSY WOKE TO SUNLIGHT streaming through her bedroom window and the feeling of having forgotten something terribly important. That wasn't unusual, really; after more than two years spent living and working in the Shop Where the Lost Things Go, it was more common for her to wake up having forgotten something than it was for her to wake up knowing everything was exactly where it was supposed to be.

Her first six months in the shop, the thing she'd forgotten was the way to get home, which should have been the simplest thing in the world: she'd passed through a single door, looking for help, and what she'd found was a whole new world, one where the rules rarely flowed the same way from one day into the next, one where most of her time was spent in the company of a talking, opinionated magpie, or wandering through the outdoor shopping plazas of impossible realities that she could never seem to find a second time, one where doors and Doors were different things. All she had to do was find her way back to the right Door and she'd be out of here, easy as anything.

Only not so much, as it turned out. No matter how many Doors she opened—and she opened a *lot* of Doors, she opened so many Doors that even Vineta was impressed—they didn't lead to anything she recognized as the world she'd come from, or even anything close to it. Worlds of talking porcelain dolls and worlds of dragons, a terrifying world filled with dinosaurs that roared and chased and sold no wares, making Vineta's claim that all the Doors opened on places with people somewhat more confusing. Another world cast entirely in black and white, where even Hudson seemed like an offensive riot of color against the monochrome sky.

After six months of Doors, Antsy had been forced to admit that she was here until she wasn't lost anymore, and so had started helping more properly with the daily operation of the shop, for the sake of earning her keep. Her keep, such as it was, seemed to be a nebulous sort of thing; both Hudson and Vineta would exclaim over how much she'd managed to buy and how good her instincts were every time she came back from a shopping trip, something that was only possible when she opened one of the Doors to get there . . . or so she thought.

She had been in her seventh month at the shop, standing behind the counter while Hudson showed her how to work the register, when a door that hadn't been there a moment before swung open in the wall across from them. It should have knocked over several shelves. It didn't. It should have been prevented from opening by the pile of broken lawn gnomes Vineta had placed against the wall, claiming they would be decorative. They weren't, and it wasn't. Instead, it opened, and a girl stepped into the shop, blinking rapidly as she tried to take in everything around her at the same time.

Antsy straightened, feeling very mature and jaded as she watched the girl approach the counter. She'd been that new and impressed once. She'd been that awed by everything around her.

She'd been a fool. "Can I help you?" she asked, once the girl was close enough.

"Oh, I hope so," said the girl, and hurried to the counter, eyes bright and oddly inhuman. Her pupils were sideways ovals, like a goat's, and not like a human's pupils at all. "My mother said that if I turned around five times and hopped on one foot while I thought very, very hard about what I wanted to find, there would be a door behind the mirror, and so I did, and then there was, and now I'm here. I've lost my kitten. Mother says when things are lost, they always end up here, and I want my kitten to come home more than anything. Please, can you help me find her?"

Antsy, who hadn't encountered anything like this before, looked hopelessly to Hudson. He ruffled his feathers the way he did when he was thinking—and wasn't it funny, how normal that had become—and said, in a thoughtful tone of voice, "Kitten. It was alive when you lost it, yes? You're not speaking of a metaphorical loss, the sort you grieve and learn from?"

"No," said the girl firmly. "My brothers were running in and out of the house like wild things, even though they know it's not allowed, and they left the front door open too long. And then, whoops and whist, my little Sparrow was gone, out into the big wide world, but alive as anything."

Hudson bobbed his head. "All right, all right, a living lost thing, then. Antsy, have you seen the menagerie section yet?"

"No," she replied, quietly confused. She'd seen all manner of things in her seven months at the shop, but nothing living apart from herself, Hudson, and Vineta.

"Then this is the thing you'll learn today," he said, sounding pleased with himself, and took off in a flurry of wings, flying in the slow, back-and-forth manner that always meant he was expecting her to follow. So she came around the side of the counter and trailed after him, the strange girl falling into step beside her.

The girl looked to be about the same age as her but, to Antsy's surprise, was considerably shorter. Maybe people weren't very tall in the world that she came from. She walked with quick, economical steps, and was wearing a simple cotton dress printed with flowers that Antsy didn't recognize, almost like daisies but with too many petals and eyes where the centers should have been. As Antsy watched, one of those flowers blinked, and she managed, barely, not to flinch away.

"Do you work here?" asked the girl, all innocence and excitement.

"I . . . I live here," said Antsy. The sentence was still unfamiliar in her mouth, like a new tooth too large for the space it had grown to fill. But like a new tooth, she knew, it would become familiar with time, until it was just a part of the shape of things, until she forgot what it was like to run her tongue over anything else.

That's one of the things about living in a body. It can change, but the ways it changes today will be the ways it has always been tomorrow. If the modification isn't noted in the moment, then it can be all too easily dismissed.

This will be important later. But it isn't important now, and it wasn't important then, as two girls and a bird moved deeper into the store.

"Oh, that must be wonderful," said the girl. "My mother says this place is a nexus, and you can go almost anywhere from here. But I can only visit. I can't stay."

Antsy, who wasn't sure how the girl thought she was going to go home again, frowned a little, and kept following the flicker of Hudson's wings. They were passing aisles she'd never seen before, each one packed with shelves and racks of clothing, each shelf and rack groaning under the weight of everything they held. This place was an endless cavern of treasures, and she could explore for a hundred years without seeing the end of it.

"They know about the Doors where you come from?" was all she asked.

"Of course," said the girl, sounding stung. "We're a *civilized* world."

Antsy didn't like what that implied about her own world, and so she didn't say anything else, just kept following Hudson until she heard something new from up ahead, something that sounded surprisingly like a dog barking. Hudson swooped around a corner. The two girls followed, and what they found there was a space that looked like a cross between the livestock barn at a state fair and an adoption event for an animal rescue. The shelves of books and knick-knacks were gone, and in their place were cages and tanks and tall habitats with multiple levels. Cats and rabbits, ferrets and rats, even dogs and foxes watched them with bright eyes. Birds rattled the bars of their cages, while snakes slithered and lizards skittered through the loam of their own tanks.

It was huge. It was impossible. It should have smelled like a barn and required daily cleaning, but somehow Antsy had never seen it before, never even suspected it might exist. It seemed ridiculous that she wouldn't have been called to feed something at least once, or asked to pick up pet food during one of their shopping trips, but here they were, and there were all the animals, and they should have had an entire staff devoted to nothing but their care. They should have been *noticeable*.

The girl made a wordless sound of delight and scurried off to look at the cages and cages of cats while Antsy stood in open-mouthed amazement. Hudson swooped toward her. She put up her arm to give him a perch, a gesture that had become so habitual that it was almost instinct by this point. He settled, claws gripping tight, and preened himself for a moment before clacking his beak in satisfaction and looking at her face.

"Well?" he asked. "What's wrong this time?"

"How is this here? I should have seen it by now. Vineta should be asking me to clean cages every day. And is that a *unicorn*?"

"It's here because animals get lost sometimes, same as anything else, and you haven't seen it because we didn't need it, and so we lost track of it."

That seemed awfully convenient, and Antsy was about to say so when a worse thought struck her. "Children get lost too," she said. "Is there an orphanage in here somewhere?"

"No! That would be ridiculous." Hudson fluffed out his feathers in annoyance. "Children get lost, but the only ones who wind up here are the ones like you, who the Doors already wanted to keep track of."

The way Hudson and Vineta talked about the Doors, they were both alive and aware. They watched people without making themselves known, and they had opinions, and they wanted things. Why they wanted the things they did, or why some worlds knew about the doors while so many others didn't, was less than clear, but all of them were somehow connected anyway. Antsy felt like there was a secret lurking just out of reach, and once she understood it, she would be able to go anywhere she wanted.

She would be able to go home. Even now, after seven months in this strange and ever-surprising place, she didn't regret what she had done; Tyler had given her what felt like no choice, and she had made the decision that was best for her in that moment. But she also missed her mother, and felt like she'd done her a disservice by disappearing so abruptly. She would be missed. She knew that without question. So eventually, no matter how much this place came to feel like home, she would need to find a way to get back.

It was only a matter of knowing how.

"So not all children need Doors?" Sometimes she asked questions that Hudson and Vineta treated as absolutely obvious, things that didn't really need asking, but it was the only way to get them to explain anything. Left to their own devices, they would say things that overturned everything she thought she knew about the way the world—any of the worlds—worked and then just walk away like it was nothing.

It wasn't nothing. It was everything.

Hudson gave her what she had come to recognize as the avian equivalent of a pitying look and said, "No. Only the ones who aren't made right for the worlds where they started out *need* Doors. All children may *want* them—who doesn't want a grand adventure? But needing and wanting aren't the same, and the Doors can see the difference. Some children need to escape from places that will only hurt them, or grind them away until they're nothing. And some children need to go somewhere else if they're ever going to grow into the people they were meant to be. The Doors choose carefully."

"So I'm special?" The idea was appealing. Who didn't want to be special?

So it was almost disappointing when Hudson ruffled his feathers and said, "Only as special as the kitten who gets picked first from a litter of twelve. It's luck as much as anything. Our Door almost always looks like a door. If you hadn't run away when you did, or if you hadn't tried to use the door you did, you wouldn't be here. The Doors have to choose you, but then you have to choose yourself. Luck and timing. Just looking for something lost doesn't make you Lost yourself."

The stranger girl was walking back toward them, a squirming ball of calico fur in her hands. "I found her!" she crowed, and held the kitten up for their approval. It squirmed in her hands, mewling and opening brown-feathered wings in frustrated feline protest.

Antsy blinked. Whatever world this girl came from, it was very different from her own. "Oh," she said, after a brief pause to reorient herself. "Well, she's lovely. Was that all you needed? You didn't lose anything else?"

"Just a shoe once, but that was when I was smaller, and it wouldn't fit me now," said the girl brightly. "I'm ready to go home."

Antsy, whose own answer would have been much longer and much more painful, felt a pang of jealousy. This girl could go home. This girl hadn't lost anything worth looking for; nothing larger than a kitten, anyway. This girl didn't know what it was to be lost herself, to feel like the world was set against her, to be hurt. This girl was innocent.

And just like that, Antsy's anger burst. This girl was innocent. This girl *could* go home. She could be safe and comfortable and cared for and unafraid. That mattered. That was something important, something worth taking care of and protecting. "I'll walk you back to your Door," said Antsy, and turned, starting back the way they had come, Hudson riding along on her arm.

The girl followed with her kitten. They had only gone a few steps when the sound of the animals behind them cut off, replaced by silence. There was no tapering off, no fading, just abrupt absence. Antsy smiled. The shop didn't think they needed the menagerie anymore, and had put it back wherever it was that it went when they forgot to look for it. Well, good. She didn't have time to take care of a pet, anyway.

The girl kept up a steady stream of nonsense conversation as they walked, commenting on everything they passed with the wide-eyed wonder of one who never expected to see anything quite so grand ever again. Antsy nodded and made accommodating noises, letting the words wash over her and not quite listening, not really. None of it mattered. The girl was going to go back to her life and her world and be safe and loved and cared for, and Antsy was going to stay here, where the lost things belonged.

When they got back to the counter, the girl's Door was still there. It hadn't disappeared the way Doors usually did when no one was looking at them. The girl bounced and waved with her free hand before running to pull the Door open, revealing a slice of green-grassed countryside on the other side. Then she ducked through, and she was gone.

Antsy looked at Hudson. "Does that happen often?"

"How often has it happened since you got here?"

"Fair enough." Antsy stepped back behind the counter. Hudson hopped off her arm and onto his perch. "You were going to show me how to work the register?"

That night, she went to bed tired but feeling oddly accomplished, like she'd done something truly important, and when she woke up in the morning, two of her baby teeth were lying on the pillow, bits of tarnished ivory, leaving empty holes in her mouth. She looked at them for a long and quiet moment before sweeping them into her hand and shoving them under the pillow, getting out of bed.

It was time for another day.

That day, they found two Doors. One led to a world filled with flowers, some of which talked, all of which were happy to accept coins of pressed fertilizer in exchange for jars of honey and pellets of nectar. Some of them sold their own perfume, and those ones delighted Vineta most of all.

The other Door led to a dark and gloomy world, with a

single red moon hanging in the sky like the eye of a baleful giant, and they did their shopping at an outdoor market built in the shadow of a terrible, looming castle like something out of a Scooby-Doo cartoon. Antsy couldn't bring herself to look at it directly, which seemed to please Vineta; none of the villagers looked directly at the castle, either, and staring would only have attracted attention.

They had been there a few hours, no more, when two girls who looked several years older than Antsy appeared, identical and opposite as sunrise and sunset. Both had golden hair and pale, pinched faces, but one was dressed like a princess out of a fairy tale, while the other was dressed like the world's youngest funeral director. The strange pair made for the stalls, and Vineta's hand clamped down on Antsy's shoulder.

"We'll be leaving now," she said, voice a quick hiss. "Come along, Antoinette."

"Are we done shopping?" she asked.

"Oh, yes. We're absolutely done." And away they went, back to the Door that led to the shop, which was hidden in a fold of shadow along the city wall. Vineta didn't relax or let go of Antsy's shoulder until they were through the door and it was shut behind them for good measure. Then she sagged, exhaling heavily.

"What was that?" demanded Antsy.

"Those were other Door-touched," said Vineta. "I don't know what world they came from, or whether it was anywhere near to yours, but you mustn't linger where the children of the Doors are already gathered. It isn't safe."

"Why not?"

"Because there aren't many nexuses like ours," said Vineta. "And most of the Door-touched want nothing more than they want to go home. They would change the world, if it meant they could go home. They're as likely as not to think they're on some sort of grand storybook adventure, and for them, saving the world and destroying it mean the same thing, as long as it comes to the same end."

Antsy blinked slowly. "But you said the Doors came for people who would be better on the other side than they were where they'd started."

"A thing being good for you doesn't make it a thing you *want*," said Vineta. "Did you like being told to eat your broccoli because it was good for you?"

Antsy frowned but had to shake her head. "No, not at all."

"To some of these travelers, the worlds the Doors offer them are broccoli. They were sure enough to pass through, and remain sure enough to stay, but part of that certainty is the conviction that until they complete their quests, they don't deserve to go home. Those girls might have ignored us as part of the scenery, or they might have recognized us as something that didn't belong and refused to let us leave. They might have followed us back to our Door, and tried to take it for their own."

"Can that *happen*? None of the people we've met in the markets have even been able to see the door we came through."

"But none of them have been Door-touched." Vineta shook her head, shifting the basket she carried to her other hand. "Those girls could have seen, and could have followed, and because this place is a nexus, being able to see the Door is enough. You don't have to be particularly called to it or tied to it for it to take you. We could have come back with two strangers in tow."

"I was a stranger when I came here," said Antsy.

"Yes, but the shop called you, even if you weren't answering an advertisement, and this is where you belong. I didn't

find you somewhere else, already mired in your own story and
resistant to changing how it would be told. Come along, now,
we have to sort our purchases and put away the perishables."

"I don't think anything's perishable except the bread and
cheese," said Antsy, and followed obediently. She had long
since learned that obedience was the easiest way to deal with
Vineta, who would spend the mornings pulling her toward
whatever Doors had appeared during the night, and then
vanish into the back for the mysterious and eternally ongo-
ing process of "inventory," which was somehow essential to
the smooth running of the shop, even though Vineta rarely
worked behind the counter or helped the occasional shoppers
who came in through more ordinary doors, usually accom-
panied by hat-wearing magpies who swooped over to chatter
excitedly with Hudson.

Once Vineta went to work on inventory, Antsy and Hudson would have the run of the shop until dinnertime. Antsy's
hands and height meant she could deal with messes and shelving issues he couldn't—and she was getting better at stretching; she could reach shelves now that had been quite out of
her reach only a few months before, and she didn't see anything odd about that, accepting it with the calm, unwavering
serenity of a child who was already under too much pressure
to notice when something was wrong. The shop itself gener-
ated tasks for them daily, piles of boxes blocking walkways
and sudden stacks of objects that needed to be put away. It
was endless, but it was easy, and even enjoyable. Antsy could
feel her arms and back growing stronger as time passed and
she became more adept at interpreting the sometimes-odd
organizational system. Hudson swooped from place to place,
grabbing small, shiny objects and tucking them where he felt

they belonged, or exclaiming with a great cacophony when he found an older cache of treasures.

And then there would be lunch, and Antsy enjoyed lunch best of all, because that was when she got to enjoy the fruits of her morning's labors, strange things from worlds she had never seen before and might never see again. Vineta joined them on days when they had returned from market with a great deal of fruit or jam, and would mutter and wave a crystal spike over each piece, watching to see what color the crystal turned. If it remained clear or turned pink or yellow, she would give the fruit to Antsy. If it turned black or red, she would keep it back.

Antsy had only asked once what the spike was for. Vineta's response had been a scowl, and a sour mutter of "No one ever misplaces a hospital," as if that somehow explained everything. Antsy thought the spike might be telling Vineta whether or not any of the things they'd brought home would hurt them in some way, and it seemed like it might be a good thing to take with them when they were doing the shopping, but as the fruit didn't seem to spoil once it was in their kitchen, and could occasionally be re-sold to people who didn't carry spikes of their own but seemed to recognize and get excited by it anyway, she supposed it was all right.

On the day when they saw the two Door-touched girls in the world with the malevolent moon, there was hard brown bread and honey that made the spike flicker between yellow and red for almost a minute before it settled on the darkest pink Antsy had ever seen, and butter so rich and delicious that it felt like every other bit of butter she'd ever tasted had just been imitating this butter and not doing a very good job of it. There had been a sausage-seller at the market, but there was no meat with the meal, and Antsy realized suddenly that Vineta had avoided all the stalls selling any sort of animal good that required the animal to be dead first—no meat, no leather, no bone dice or jerky. It was a small but uncommon omission.

She squinted at Vineta, who continued buttering a slice of toast and ignored her. There was no meat, but there *was* cheese, as fine as the butter, sharp and crumbly and so delicious that it felt almost like a sin to swallow, like the flavor was a living thing that should have been allowed to linger on the tongue forever if that was its heart's desire.

But even the most delicious cheese must eventually be eaten, and when the last of lunch was put away, Vineta vanished again, and Antsy and Hudson had the run of the store.

Nothing else about that afternoon or evening stood out in Antsy's memory: it had been a day like any other, once they were past lunch, and she'd gone to bed once again content with the things she had done and the choices she had made. And it never even occurred to her that she hadn't spent any time looking for the Door that would take her home.

The next morning when she woke, her calves hurt. She had to rub them for almost a solid minute before she got out of bed, and they still felt odd as she walked to the bathroom and reached for her toothbrush. She was halfway through brushing her teeth when she realized the holes left by her baby teeth were gone; her adult teeth had finished growing overnight, and fit smoothly into her mouth. She bared her teeth at the mirror, studying her reflection, trying to see the shape of her adult smile in her reflection. It wasn't quite there yet, but it felt like it was coming, like the bones of her face were rearranging themselves to prepare for the woman she was going to be. Antsy dropped her toothbrush back into its cup with a feeling of solemn satisfaction and scampered back to her room to check under her pillow.

The lost teeth were gone, replaced by two large chocolate coins and a note with a shelf location written in unfamiliar handwriting, and under that, a single sentence:

Nothing comes free; ask them what it costs you.

The note wasn't signed. Antsy frowned and put it on the dresser while she turned to put on her clothes for the day, and the stirring of the air from pulling off her nightgown was enough to send the note tumbling behind the dresser, where she promptly forgot about it. Not in the casual way of forgetting things when they lack importance; no, this was a forgetting so profound that the thing forgotten might as well never have existed. She'd lost nothing. There had been nothing to lose.

The chocolate coins were still on her pillow. She snatched them as she ran out of the room, and she didn't look back.

It wouldn't be until a morning almost two years later, when all her remaining baby teeth had been bought and paid for with chocolate, and no more mysterious notes, that she would even remember that she'd lost something.

By that point, it would almost be too late.

8 WHAT WE LOSE ALONG THE WAY

ON THE MORNING WHEN Antsy woke feeling as if she'd forgotten something, she had been sleeping in the little room at the top of the shop for two years. Two years since she'd run away from home and stumbled through a door and found herself pressed into a job she was only just beginning to think she truly understood. Two years of strange new worlds almost every day—sometimes several times a day; her record was eleven, and that had left her not only frustrated by how little she'd been able to see of each world but also so exhausted and disoriented that she'd gone to bed and slept for almost an entire week, after which Hudson had put his talon down with Vineta and restricted her to a maximum of five Doors a day. Antsy had been grateful but sorry; the markets were her favorite part of the day, and their constant variety kept her from getting bored when so much time was spent on sorting and shelving.

She sometimes felt as if she was missing something, not attending a traditional school, but she could read and write well enough to enjoy the storybooks she sometimes found written in English, and a handful of words and phrases in a hundred other languages. She could make change in three dozen currencies, and carry a basket that weighed half as much as she did. She could even navigate the shop without help, and did so most days, spending the first part of her mornings hunting through the shelves for Doors that had appeared in the night. It had taken her most of the first year to learn that she should just make note of their locations and not attempt to open them; every turn of the knob unlocked another world, and she had lost many promising markets and tempting fields before she'd realized she should leave them alone while she fetched Vineta.

She had been seven going on eight when she found the Shop Where the Lost Things Go, and now she was nine going on ten. She had a very good sense of how long it had been, both thanks to the calendars she sometimes found on the shelves and her own accounting of the days. she knew how long she'd been here, and how long her mother had been waiting to see her again. Two years. One day she would find the Door that took her home. One day.

But until then, she had a job to do, and because she had been here so long, she didn't find it entirely odd that she had grown during those two years. If there had been anyone around for her to compare herself to apart from Vineta, she might have realized something was wrong, but with only an ancient woman and a bird to measure herself against, it didn't seem all that strange that she had gone from a perfectly reasonable four feet to almost five and a half feet in height over the course of just two years.

Some of the other changes had been more of a surprise. When she'd woken up with blood on her sheets, Vineta had sat her down for a halting, uncomfortable conversation about babies and the making of them, and how to handle cramping and cleaning up after herself. She'd finished that conversation with a critical look at the full length of Antsy, and a muttered "I thought we'd be doing this sooner, with you being nine when you first got here. But I suppose longer is better, in the main stretch of things." And then she'd sent Antsy upstairs, restricted from her duties for the day.

There had been a basket of sanitary products in the bathroom that day, and an assortment of herbal teas in her bedroom, ready to be brewed, as well as a drawer filled with new underpants and several training bras that fastened at the back and relieved a pressure Antsy had barely noticed building in her chest. And since, again, she had no one to compare herself to, she hadn't really noticed that other things were changing perhaps faster than they really should have.

The girl who left her room, paused, and turned to walk back inside, was almost three months shy of her tenth birthday, and she had the face and figure of a girl well past the age of sixteen, cruising through her teen years and cresting toward adulthood.

The feeling that she'd forgotten something was still there, pressing down on her, making it difficult to think about breakfast or doors or stocking or any of the other things that should have been occupying her mind by now. She stopped in the middle of her bedroom and turned a slow, deliberate circle, allowing her thoughts to go blurry and unfocused.

The feeling of something being forgotten was often a message from the shop itself, an attempt at communication by something essentially voiceless. She'd learned to listen, over the years. That seemed to be the key, the thing that made it all better. Listening.

Her eyes caught on something white under the dresser, down among the dust bunnies and the tiny feathers that Hudson sometimes lost during his infrequent molts. He'd done it four times since she'd come to the shop, and every time he was left unable to fly for weeks, petulant and unhelpful as he sulked on his perch. She usually swept up after a molt, but it wasn't odd for her to miss a few bits of downy fluff.

Still, it was odd for a feather big enough to see to get forgotten. Antsy dropped to her knees. Maybe it was a sock. Lost socks were incredibly common in the shop and could appear virtually anywhere, not just in the stock rooms in the back. It was like there were so many that the shop couldn't channel them all the way it was supposed to. They disappeared just as quickly, popping in and out of view as people found them in the ordinary way.

Two years, and Antsy still wasn't entirely clear on the mechanism by which items could vanish on their own, called back to the place where they'd begun without the shortcut of shopping in a place filled with other things just like them, things that might be waiting for their owners to come and reclaim them. She'd learned to hear the hum of the shop telling her an item was safe to sell, that its owner had replaced it or forgotten it or otherwise moved on, and when she didn't find it, she would offer something else instead, preserving the things that still might be come for like flies in amber.

Her questing fingers didn't find a sock or a feather under the dresser. Instead, they brushed against a piece of paper. She pulled it out into the light, squinting at what was written there. She remembered it, vaguely, like it was something she'd read once in a dream.

Nothing comes free; ask them what it costs you.

The urge to put it back under the dresser was swift, and so heavy that she began the motion before she realized what was happening. Antsy scowled, balling her hand into a fist with the paper caught inside. "No," she informed the ceiling. "I know you want this to be lost, and I don't understand why, but I don't care, either. You're a store, you don't get to tell me what to do."

Then she stood, and the air was heavy around her, pressing down, like the store could absolutely tell her what to do if it wanted to, and she was being the unreasonable one by trying to say it couldn't. Antsy brushed it off with the grace that came from long practice as she left the room and descended the stairs.

Hudson and Vineta weren't up yet. Both of them were inclined to stay abed longer than she was, which Vineta blamed on having old bones and Hudson blamed, more frankly, on being a lazy bird. Antsy checked the paper again, making silent note of the shelf location written at the top, and began to walk.

It took a while. Near as she could tell, the shop was close to infinite, filled with aisles and tiny rooms that only existed when someone needed them. The door to the yard was on the other side of the employee area, and the yard itself was easily as large as the shop it was attached to. Antsy was normally careful not to go too deep, out of the genuine fear that if she did, she might not be able to find her way back without sending up a flare or starting a fire or something.

Hudson always seemed to know exactly where the things he was looking for were located. He had an innate sense of the shop's geography and current stock levels that Antsy assumed was connected to this being his world of origin. He had started out here; of course he understood it, the way she assumed she would slide back into the world she'd left without missing a beat when she finally got to go home. You knew the place you came from.

But something told her that going back to fetch Hudson wouldn't do her any good, that it wouldn't find the thing she was looking for or make her search any easier. It was such an odd feeling that she focused on it as she walked past aisles filled with things she didn't recognize, things made for use in worlds other than her own. Who could possibly have used a sword made of candy glass, so brittle it would shatter as soon as someone swung it, breaking without doing any real damage? Or a harp made of bones? That one was unsettling. Antsy shuddered and walked faster, leaving it behind, until she finally reached the section the note had indicated.

This space was . . . odd. The shelves were dusty, which didn't happen in even the most underused parts of the shop; even when no one went there, the shop kept itself clean, within the limits of its ill-defined ability. They were as crowded with items as any other shelf she might have wanted to examine, but they didn't seem to make any sense. They weren't grouped by category, or by color, and even the assumption that they were sorted by world of origin didn't survive glancing at more than one of the shelving units. Each shelf seemed to consist only of items from a single world, but each unit had at least six shelves, and since she was finally tall enough to reach the highest of them—which felt odd and utterly natural at the same time; she'd been the one who lived with all that growth, day by day, and so it should be perfectly reasonable for her to reach the top shelves.

And each shelf in each unit held things that clearly came from a different world. Antsy picked up a plush rabbit, knocking loose a cloud of dust, and almost dropped it as a new feeling swept over her, one she'd never gotten before, from anything.

It wasn't lost. It knew exactly where its owner was, and it had no desire to be handled by anyone else. Antsy forced her fingers to stay locked in place, mostly because if she dropped it, she wasn't sure she'd be able to pick it up again. It kept radiating the feeling that she was doing something wrong, that she had no right, no authority, no *reason* to be touching it in the first place. But she didn't want to leave it on the floor to get kicked under a shelf and forgotten, and that was what would happen if she let go. She breathed in and out through her nose, trying to understand the frozen disdain coming off the stuffed bunny, and finally found what felt like an answer. The rabbit's owner was dead, lost to the dust and the silence, but that owner was somehow still in the shop. The rabbit wasn't lost, had never *been* truly lost, because its owner had always known exactly where it was.

Antsy shivered and put it back where she'd found it, looking at the rest of the shelf. The first few items were like the rabbit, a little worn and tattered, but well loved and used by the hands of their person. After that, things became more impersonal, more like icons of events than actual reminders of them. A small, tarnished brass trophy. A photo album she didn't quite dare to touch. A stick of unburnt incense. It was very odd.

The last item on the shelf was a glass jar filled to the brim with human teeth. The ones at the bottom were small and white, children's lost teeth, and the ones at the top were larger, worn and yellowed, like they'd come from the mouth of an adult. Antsy shuddered and turned her attention to the next shelf down.

It was the same story: small personal items fading into icons, teeth at the end. And the shelf beneath it, and the one beneath that, and all the shelves around her, hundreds of them stretching out into forever. She looked around, wide-eyed, trying to figure out what this section could possibly represent.

Her directions had included a shelf as well as a section. Suddenly direly afraid she didn't want to know, she uncrumpled the note and began counting her way along the units toward the one she'd been sent to find. It was most of the way to the end of the row. The unit looked just like all the others, and then Antsy saw the shelf and stopped being able to catch her breath.

The first item was her backpack, the one she'd been carrying when she fell through the shop door, and how had it gotten here? It was covered by a thick layer of dust and had clearly been here for quite some time, and as she stared at it, she realized she couldn't remember when she'd lost it. Next to it was a shoe, one of the ones she'd been wearing on that first day. It looked impossibly small, like it could never have encompassed her foot. Next to it was a coin from the first Door she'd actually gone through intentionally, the Door into Dejanira, and a little tuft of blue-purple fur. That should have pinged as being from a different world than the backpack and the shoe, but it felt like everything else around it, like it belonged where it was, a part of this set. She realized she couldn't trust the shelves to be telling her the truth about where their contents had come from, and she worried her lip between her teeth for a moment before reaching out and brushing her fingertips against the coin.

It wasn't lost; like the bunny, it was still tethered to its owner, and was precisely where it belonged. But it didn't radiate rejection or the feeling she needed to take her hand away. Instead, it welcomed her touch like it was coming home, and when she closed her eyes, she saw the market, saw herself walking with Sákos, and the last two years had been so wild and strange that it wasn't the sight of the human-sized feline that caused her to yank her hand away from the coin, shattering the memory that had been more like a movie, herself seen from the outside.

No, it wasn't Sákos. It was the little girl next to him, the *child*.

She was still a child, she *was,* she was nine years old, but the girl in her vision was so impossibly small that it was like being told she'd gone from a sapling to a tree in just two years. Hand shaking, Antsy reached out and touched the coin again. There was no second vision. Almost frantic now, she grabbed for the next item on the shelf—a pencil with tooth-marks deeply etched into the wood—and gasped when she saw herself again, taller than she'd been in the previous snap-shot, but still obviously so much younger than she had looked in the mirror that morning. She pulled her hand away and looked at the rest of the shelf.

It was sparse compared to the shelves around it, no more than a quarter full, and every item recognizable. At the very end of the line was a small jar, like all the others, its base covered by a layer of tiny white teeth. All of them were baby teeth, and there were so many of them. Her adult teeth had always come in so quickly that she'd never really stopped to think about how fast she was losing them, but it had been *very* fast, hadn't it? She couldn't remember the last time she'd had a tooth to lose. She ran her tongue around the inside of her mouth, feeling the now-familiar topography of her adult teeth. No, that part of her growing was done, even though it shouldn't have been.

She should have *noticed*. If she'd somehow . . . if she was that much bigger than she should have been, if she had grown up in the span between seconds, she should have known about it. She reached for the jar, grabbing it like it would somehow give her the answers she so desperately desired.

Touching it was like sticking her finger into a live electrical socket. Static raced through her, painful and sharp and some-how cousin to the resistance she felt whenever she opened a door, and she saw. She saw two years of moments in an in-stant, two years that had somehow swallowed nine.

That time was lost. She dropped the jar of teeth back onto the shelf. It landed on its side and rolled, spraying tiny white teeth from its mouth in a shallow arc. She took a step back, hyperventilating, clutching her hand to her chest, and almost recoiled when it pressed against the slope of her breasts. She'd grown them at least a year ago, a process that had been swift and remarkably painful, resulting in waking up almost every morning with skin that felt like it had been yanked on in the night and aches in the muscle all the way down to her ribcage, and while they'd been annoying at first, she'd adjusted to their presence with remarkable speed.

Everything since she'd arrived here had happened with remarkable speed. It hurt to think too hard about that now.

Nothing comes free; ask them what it costs you.

Suddenly, it was obvious what it had cost her, although she wasn't entirely sure how. She took a deep, shuddering breath, gaze dipping lower, to the shelf below the one that was so obviously hers.

It began with a small, withered bundle of dried flowers, and continued on from there, trinkets and artifacts from dozens of worlds, and at the end, the little jar of teeth, this one with only a few small baby teeth at the bottom and then so many adult teeth above it. Antsy chewed her lip as she cataloged the artifacts with her eyes, not quite daring to touch them. There was less dust on this shelf, like someone still came to clean it from time to time. Like it was remembered.

Those flowers, withered as they were, weren't half as ancient as they should have been. She remembered the market where Vineta had bought them. Shoving the note that had started this whole thing into the depths of her pocket, Antsy put her hands over her face, and she cried.

PART IV

HOW TO GET FOUND

9 REVENGE OF THE LOST THINGS

EVENTUALLY, ANTSY'S TEARS RAN out, as tears will always do, and a bright new anger built under her ribs, growing and swelling like a poisonous flower until it felt like it would split her skin and leave her broken on the floor. She wiped her cheeks with the flats of her hands and went storming back the way she had come, only to find herself confronted with an endless maze of shelves, none of them familiar.

She hadn't been so lost in the shop since the first days she was here, and she resented it. Planting her hands on her hips, she tilted her head toward the shadowy ceiling and demanded, "What do you want me to do? There's no one else who could have left that note, so I know it was you who wanted me to find this place. Well, why? I didn't know. I could have gone on not knowing for a long time."

And she could have; that was the tragedy of it all. Maybe that seemed unreasonable, and it would have been if there'd been anyone around to compare herself to, or if her mother had been there to cluck her tongue and comment on how tall Antsy was getting, but alone and with nothing to measure against, Antsy had taken her rate of growth and maturation as perfectly reasonable, perfectly ordinary, the same things she would have experienced if she'd never run away from home. Now . . .

Now she felt violated, stolen from, *robbed*. She should have had a childhood, ice cream and matinees and sunshine and cookies, not working in a dusty shop while she grew up faster than she should have been able to, rocketing toward adulthood, spending hours she'd never be able to recover! She should have had *time*. It was hers, and she had never agreed to give it away.

"They were supposed to tell you," said a voice from behind her. Antsy turned. There was a girl, as human as she was, except for the delicate moth's wings of her eyelashes, the feathered antennae that rose from her forehead, and the tattered remains of actual wings that hung from her shoulders, too broken to ever have been used to fly. She was so small, so tiny and delicate, and Antsy realized she was thinking of the girl as an impossibly young child when she looked like she was the same age Antsy was actually supposed to be.

It stung.

"I didn't know, when I made this place," said the girl, walking to one of the longer shelves, shadowed and choked in dust and cobwebs. She reached into its depths, and her hand passed straight through those cobwebs, not disturbing them in the least. Antsy realized she could see through the girl, just a little, just enough to make it clear that she wasn't really here. Not the way Antsy was.

As if hearing that realization, the girl glanced back at Antsy, a wry smile on her half-visible face, even as she pulled a small black notebook out of the recesses of the shelf. "I really didn't. I'd been running away from home—I had a very good reason to be running—and I found a door that dumped me into a tiny little wooden room. It's your bedroom now. The rest of the shop came later. When I opened the door and looked outside, it was junk in piles as far as the eye could see, with doors jammed in them at random. I opened one, thinking it would take me home, and saw a whole new world. It was . . ." She paused, bracing herself, and took a deep breath before she said, "It was magical. It was everything I'd ever wanted, and I never, ever wanted to go home."

"Why did you run away?"

"It was . . . it was bad." The girl turned back to Antsy. "I had two sisters before me, and both of them died before they were grown, and no one would ever say why, only that they were gone from me. And then my first mother bore my father a son, a strong boy, and everyone said he would live, and I guess that was all he'd been waiting to hear. He started hitting me that same night. He broke my wings, so badly they never straightened again, and I would never be able to fly upon my own majority. I would have no husband or household of my own, and still he didn't stop, and still my mothers didn't defend me. I knew if I stayed, I would die." She looked at Antsy with wise, weary eyes. "You must have known something similar, to find my door."

Antsy looked away, unable to face that searching gaze. "Similar enough," she said. "He never hit me, but I don't think he needed to."

"No. They don't, always." The girl offered Antsy her notebook. "This is for you, now. They should have told you. They were supposed to tell you. That was what the doors and I agreed on, back in the beginning, when all this was new."

"The Doors can talk?" The girl didn't say the word the way Antsy had learned to, didn't put the emphasis on it as a proper noun: she said "door" like it was a normal thing, a tool, and not some all-powerful force.

It sounded kinder.

"Not exactly, but they communicate, in their way, if you know how to listen." She pressed the notebook into Antsy's hands. "I built this place board by board to give the things I found a little dignity until their owners came back for them, and a place to rest if their owners never came. I wanted it to be safe here. For kids like me. And that wanting went into the walls, and they came, so many of you, over and over, and it broke my heart every time, even though I'm dead and gone and only lingering because I lost the right to be buried in the halls of my own people. And sometime along the way, the adults who had been lost children stopped telling the new arrivals the truth of the tolls. It was wrong. It was unfair. I had to figure it out on my own, but I was in an empty world, no shop, no system, no one telling me what to do or how to do it. It's easy to go along with a system. It's harder to create one. You have to choose it, over and over, when you're building it. You should have been told. All of you should have been told.

"But I'm not here anymore. I'm as lost as you are. It's hard for me to say anything, and it took me a long time and a lot of effort to send that note, and after I did, I had to sleep for a while, so I didn't realize you'd lost it. The shop and I don't always agree anymore. I'm gone and it's still here, and it needs you, in a way that it no longer needs me."

"What were they supposed to tell me?"

"It's in the book," said the girl, moth-winged eyelids drooping. She looked tired. She looked like she was aging in front of Antsy's eyes, almost as tall as Antsy herself now, and Antsy realized she'd been talking to her as she was when she first got here, before she had . . . died, presumably, and now she was getting older, aging at a rapid clip. Her hair, colorless in its translucency, grew straight and stringy; her skin grew thin and seamed.

"What was your name?" asked Antsy, anxious to learn more before the girl—no, woman, now—before she disappeared, and Antsy was alone again.

"Elodina," said the woman, and sighed. "I wish I could have flown. I wish you had been warned. I'm sorry."

And then she was gone, but the notebook remained, and the feeling it radiated was not of loss, but of being found; this thing belonged to Antsy now.

Sitting down on the floor with her back against the nearest shelf, Antsy opened the tiny book and began to read.

10 IN A TIME OF MISTS AND MOTHS

THE TEXT WAS SMALL and slanting, and Antsy recognized the handwriting immediately as matching the note she'd found under her dresser. It seemed to swim in front of her eyes for a moment, translating itself from a language she didn't know into easy English. Years without formal schooling had left her not quite as skilled a reader as she might have been, but she'd been old enough to be reading chapter books when she ran away, and so once she focused and concentrated, the words unsnarled themselves.

"Cyane is dead. Mother says it was an accident, but I am less than sure. She was a strong and clever flier; she knew the winds and how they would treat her under any safe condition, and she would not fly during a storm. But the babe is healthy and well, and Father says we are not to taint this time of joy with mourning. The babe will carry our family's name into the future on broad and cunning wings, and we will not lose our place when our father's time is done. We should all be grateful for his arrival. We should all be glad.

"But I am not grateful. I am not glad. My sister is dead. She will never brush my hair or bring me sugared fruits again. She will not sing to me at night, or praise me in the morning. My sister is dead, and no one will mourn her but me . . ."

The rest of the page was more of the same, the rambling grief of a little girl who had lost what mattered most to her in the world. Antsy recognized the emotions all too well; they had been her own, on that long-ago day when her father fell in the Target toy aisle.

She hadn't thought about that day in years. She shuddered, as much out of shared sorrow for a girl she'd never known as from the shame of realizing how much she'd allowed to fade away into the misty halls of memory. Flipping ahead several pages, she skimmed the text, looking for the place where Elodina's story began colliding with her own.

She found it about a quarter of the way in.

"My wings are broken such that they will not heal. Father says I am a burden to the family, as if he were not the one to have the breaking of them. Father says a daughter who cannot fly and cannot wed brings nothing to the halls of her family, carries no value, contains no future. He will not even consider me for the weavers or for the halls of education; I am a shame and a betrayal of his own virility. I should not have been born a girl. I should not have been made weak by the love of my mothers and sister. I should not have allowed myself to be swayed from my duty. But I did all those things, and now, for that crime, I am to die. There is no question in my heart but that he intends to kill me.

"I am strangely calm in the face of my own destruction. He has beaten me enough, and he will be kinder to both my mothers and to Mitrofan if I am gone. But still, I find I do not wish to die. I may never fly again, and still there are winds I have never tasted, fires I have never seen, and I yearn for them. I wish to be free of this fate that I did nothing to bring upon myself, did nothing to earn. So I will go.

"There is little enough here which belongs to me. I will take it all, and it will be no more than I can carry, even if I must descend to the ground. Better to be devoured in the dark than to stay and be destroyed by a man who has every reason to love and care for me. He has no right to do as he has done. Let that be the crime for which I am finally convicted: my father is not a good man, and I will not pretend he is, will not praise him in ways he has not earned and never will. So I go tonight, alone, into the dark, and only hope I will survive it . . ."

Antsy skipped forward again, only a few pages this time, stopping when she caught the word "door" at the top of the page. She paused, frowning, and began to read again.

". . . strange door led me to a room such as I have never seen before. The top of it is closed, not open to the sky as a proper room would be, and there is a glass shield over the window, preventing anyone who sleeps here from leaping out into the wind. It is solid and secure, and I think I will be safe here. The wound in my arm is beginning to scab over, and will be healed soon."

So she had been injured somewhere in the intervening pages. Antsy almost flipped back, but pressed forward at the last second, more desperate to know what *would* happen than what *had* happened.

"It seems I am in an entirely new place, for when I open the door that led me here, it does not connect to the forest I left, but to a vast field filled with discarded items. They feel lost to me, as if they have been somehow taken from their proper owners. They wish to be returned. Doors dot the piles, common as red flowers in the fields of home, and I wonder where they might lead . . ."

A line break, and then:

"The doors lead to other worlds, each and every one of them. I opened one which showed an ocean such as Mother used to speak of. I had never seen an ocean before. I was afraid this door might behave as the one which brought me here, and so I wedged it open with a stone before stepping through. The air pushed back against me for but a moment, and when I stood on the shell-speckled sand, the scab on my arm was all but gone, days of healing accomplished in an instant. I stared at it for a time, then gathered the loveliest of the shells I could see and carried them back through the door with me. The wound on my arm, though diminished, remained, and did not make any further improvements on the return journey. I must consider this."

A new page before:

"I have begun building walls to allow me to sort and clean the things that were here when I arrived. The walls seem to expand in the night while I am sleeping, as if a swarm of helpful bees is coming to construct its hive of wood and nails. I am not yet very skilled with a hammer, but these things deserve to be treated with some modicum of respect. They have hearts. I can feel them beating. So I will build them a home and haven, as none was built for me, and I will care for them as long as I am able."

The next several paragraphs were about construction. Antsy skimmed them before settling on:

"The black-and-white birds that fill the skies here have taken an interest in what I do. They say this is the Land Where the Lost Things Go, and that it is a nexus of worlds, of which there are a number beyond counting. It pulls all lost things to it, and that includes the doors, which would normally wander freely. They come here when they have no children to call to them, taking a time to rest and recover themselves. The magpies, lacking hands, have never been able to open the doors themselves, but the children who sometimes come through them can.

"I am the first such child to have both arrived and stayed. Most arrive, look around at the scattered piles of lost things, find something that already belongs to them, and rush to reclaim it, carrying it with them back through their door. The magpies say they have been waiting for me, or for someone like me, to be chosen by the doors to stay and help them. They will assist me in constructing a home for all these things which we must protect."

Another skipped line, and then:

"The doors are moving. My shelter is but half-constructed, and when I woke this morning, there were two doors along the wall. I studied them a time before I went looking for something sharp, and found a silver blade in a pile of old shoes. Choosing the rightmost door, I made a cut along the back of my hand, opened the door, and walked through it with the wound still bleeding. When I arrived on the other side, it was with a cut scabbed over and clean as if it had been healing under ideal circumstance for two full days. A similar cut made before returning did not heal in the same fashion. I am thus sure of what it costs to play at being a key to another world: two full days of time.

"It is a small thing, to forfeit two days for such wonders as I saw on the other side of that door, and the next one, and the next. Wonders and delights beyond all measure, beyond counting, beyond consideration. I will have my fill of all the universe, and perhaps a sufficiency of days may give my wings the time they need to straighten and heal. Perhaps I can have the sky again, if I take time enough."

Several pages had been ripped out of the little notebook after that, disappearing completely, and the next page began with four words, sharply underlined:

"<u>I was a fool.</u>

"Two days is nothing. Two days is a bad bit of fish and a necessary lie-in. Two days is negligible. But when there are doors every day, new worlds to explore, and the fee is always the same . . . it adds up. It adds up so quickly. If you are reading this, if you are one of those who will come after me, please, believe me in this if you believe nothing else: it adds up, and what you pay will never be returned. This is the place where all things are found, but what is lost here is truly lost forever.

"I have frittered away years in the course of months. *Years.* And those years are gone; they will not be recovered, not now, not ever, no matter how much I might wish that they could be. I am a woman now, as I was a child when I arrived here, and my shop is yet half-built, and more magpies arrive to help me every day. They filter through the piles of lost things, they help me find the ones that may one day be reclaimed, and they bring me what food they can carry. They help me. They know I may never find the door which leads back to my own world, and that if I did find it, taking it would do me no good; the elders of my hive would expect a child just approaching the first flushes of her metamorphosis, broken-winged and small, but good for greater growth. They would not recognize me as I am. They would push me away as a stranger to them, and by my body, I am, but by my heart, I have left them less than a year ago.

"I will see this place completed. I will see the walls sound and the roofs secure. I will see the lost things of a universe cared for and protected. I will not see much more. It seems like such a small, enormous thing to have spent a lifetime on, and I have spent it so much faster than I had ever expected. But the magpies offer me some company, and at least I sleep knowing I am not alone . . ."

Another skipped line, and then:

"It is so hard, to stay away from the doors, even knowing what they represent. I find myself looking at them with longing every time I bruise my shin or jam my finger. They bring me wonders and glories and revelations beyond price, but there *is* a price, and I know how old my people can be before we fade and fall. I am already as aged as my grandmother was when she died of time's weight. My own grave is not too far from me. I must not be tempted, however vast the temptation may be become. I must endure. I *will* endure, for the work must still be done. All these things, how they sing to me, how they need to be cared for until they can be found again . . . the work must still be done. I want nothing more than to go through door after door until there is no more of me, to see the universe spread out before me like the fruits on a tree, each unique and each connected, part of the same whole. I cannot. I owe this place my service, for even as it has stolen my time away, I gave it freely, and the door that brought me here did so to save me.

"Had I realized the cost sooner, I could have returned home, transformed enough to be a stranger, but also safe from my father's wrath, for he would never have dared lay hands on a woman he was not related to, even one whose wings were broken in the same manner as his distaff daughter's. This could have been a gift, had I only used it more wisely. That I did not is my burden, and not the fault of the doors."

Antsy looked up from the page, eyes aching from so much unfamiliar reading, and stared into the distant shadows of the shop, trying to decide how she felt about that. Was this really something that could be blamed on an inattentive child betrayed by wonders, unable to resist one more piece of cake even when they knew it might lead to a stomachache and a sleepless night? Should she have been more aware, and not trusted Vineta, the only adult she had access to, to tell her things were changing more rapidly than they should have been?

Taking a deep breath, she looked back down at the notebook.

"A new child has appeared! Like me, he came through the door and it slammed behind him, disappearing as I watched. Like me, he was fleeing from an adult who would do him harm.

"And like me, he is trapped here. He cannot go back to where he was. But he is young—so young—and I have told him how the doors work. I have explained their function, and what they will cost him to use. He has decided he can spare a little time, if it means access to such magic as I have offered him, and his own adventure is begun.

"He brings back fruit and bread and sweet jams from truly foreign lands, and he helps me build with the vigor and the eagerness of youth. Already he is learning to sort through the debris to find the gems, the things we must tend after, and he is careful to record his passages so he knows how much time is being spent. He may be able to survive this long enough to find his own door home . . ."

More missing pages, then, until the narrative resumed with:

"I am a foolish old woman. It hurts me to say such things, but the truth is often a blade on which to cut yourself, and I have been cut deeply. Today, I was working on what will be the stock room when we are finished, when my hammer slipped and struck my hand full-on, hard enough to break bones. We were able to set them immediately, pressing them into a cast, but the pain was so bad I thought I might die.

"The child—who is a child no longer, and thus has earned a name: the young man who calls himself Eider, opened a door and pulled me through, intending to reduce the swelling. It did not change. I understand now something I had not understood before: only the one who opens the door will pay the toll. Anyone else who passes through a door once opened will do so unaffected. I can still see the universe, so long as I do it upon Eider's heels. I have spent my own reserves, but as long as he still travels, the worlds are not closed to me. This is dangerous knowledge. Novelty is addictive. I can see where one might be tempted to allow the next child to proceed in ignorance, to spend their days like they mean nothing, all for the sake of opening the universe to those whose time has already passed them by.

"That must not be allowed to happen. I have told Eider what I understand, and made him promise to tell whoever comes after him, to make sure they understand before they open a single door of their own. He swore he would never be one who abused children as he had been abused; he would allow no one to act without understanding what it might cost them.

"When I die, which will not be as far from now as I would wish it to be, this place will be left in good hands. Eider will guard the doors, and the magpies will help him manage the shop we have made together. It will be safe. I think, as it grows, that it is becoming aware, much as the doors are, much as this world is. It knows us, and it grows under our caring hands. It is the only explanation for the way it expands. We work through the days, sometimes pausing to travel together through a door that Eider opens, and we sleep through the nights, and when we wake, the shop is larger. Shelves build themselves without our aid; rooms appear. I think it has always been here in potential, only waiting for hands such as ours to come along and put a shape to it.

"It has been waiting so long for the opportunity to exist, but even as I avoid opening the doors myself, my time dwindles day by day, moving at the normal pace of things. My kind live shorter lives than Eider's; he wears the marks of his days much less openly than I wear mine, and I will leave him soon. I only plan to wait until I have so few days remaining that I can count them on the fingers of one hand, and then I will open a final door.

"I will go through it, and I will rest.

"It will be very nice, to rest."

There was one more open line, and then a new handwriting took up the narrative, blockier, heavier, easier to read:

"Elodina is gone. She opened a door this morning, and upon seeing that the other side was a vast and tangled forest like the ones she had described from her childhood, she sighed, and bid me to be careful in the remainder of my time here, and stepped through. The toll thus paid, I followed her, and helped her into the shadow of a great tree, where she sat and closed her eyes and held my hand until her breath stopped, and she was over. The great tale of her being shall be extended no more; she is gone to the Library where all of us must one day be Returned, and she will pay no overdue fines on her soul.

"But I will miss her so very much. She was my first and only friend, and I am lost without her."

Antsy sniffled, dragging the back of her hand across her cheeks, which were wet with streaky tears. Elodina had died long before she arrived here—it was impossible to say how long ago, with the apparent age of the store and the way the doors ate time—but still, she felt she knew her now, and it was easy to grieve for her. For what she'd lost, and what she'd found, and the fact that they had never been able to be children together.

Returning her attention to the book, she read on:

"A girl came through one of the doors today, and it closed behind her. She has a broken arm and she screamed herself awake when she tried to sleep. I think she will be staying for a while. Her name is Anya, and she yearns for safety. I can offer her that.

"I have told her what the doors demand, and she is young yet; she sees no danger in the exchange. Time for travel is a tempting bargain to her. I have few enough doors remaining to me, but if she will open them while her time is long, then it will not matter that my time grows short. We can continue our work. The sorting of the things behind the shop requires only our effort, and the travel to other worlds repays us in food and drink and wonders.

"We can be happy here. This is Elodina's book, and this is the last I will write within it. Her story ended with her; let me return her accounting to the shelf the shop has made for her. It has made another such for me, and I believe Anya will have a shelf soon, if it is not there already. We were lost and now we have been found, and that is more than good enough for a man like me."

There was nothing more. Antsy stood, looking down the row of shelving units, each one containing multiple shelves, each shelf packed with mementos of someone who had spent all their time here. Slowly, she put the book back where it belonged and turned toward the aisle.

She and Vineta were going to have a conversation, and if

she didn't like the way it went, she was done here. She would open one more door, and she would allow it to close behind her, and she would be gone.

All she needed was to know.

11 A CONVERSATION AND A CONCLUSION

HUDSON WAS ALREADY AT the counter when Antsy came stalking out of the aisles, her chin down and her hands balled into fists. Years of working around bipeds had left Hudson better keyed to their moods and expressions than most birds, and he ruffled his feathers in dismay at the look on her face.

"Er, Antsy?" he said. "Is something wrong?"

"Where's Vineta?"

"It's early yet; we have inventory to do before it's time to go gathering for the day. She's not going to be up for hours. Surely whatever you need to talk to her about can . . . wait . . ."

Antsy cocked her head, eyes growing dark with unexpressed storms. "Elodina mentioned black-and-white birds," she said. "She meant you and your people, didn't she? The magpies who live here? Who come from this world? She knew you. Do you remember her? Do you have a counting rhyme about her, and Eider, and Anya, and all the other shopkeepers?"

Hudson shivered. "We do," he admitted, voice small.

"Teach it to me."

Hudson huddled on his perch, feathers puffed out until he was almost a sphere, and said nothing.

"You have a little rhyme for everything, you're the accountant, so why can't you teach me *this* rhyme, huh? What's so different about it that it needs to be a secret? Unless it's full of things you decided I didn't need to know. When did you stop telling us? When did you decide that since we were already lost, it didn't matter if you used us up and threw us away? Huh? Huh?"

"Young lady, you will stop that at once," said a voice from behind her. Antsy stiffened and turned, slowly, until she was facing Vineta. The old woman leaned on her cane and scowled at Antsy. "Hudson has done nothing to deserve your ire, and it is quite unfair of you to subject him to it."

"Did *you* know?" demanded Antsy.

"When I first arrived? No. I didn't. Elodina slipped me a note on what should have been my seventeenth birthday, but was actually closer to my twenty-third, and I found her shade walking the curator's shelves, all but faded away. I thought the meddlesome thing had spent the last of her energy on trying to convince me to run. If I'd even suspected she might reach out to you, I would have done so many things differently. But we always see the past more clearly than we see the future, and she has done you no favors."

Rage tightened Antsy's skin and blurred her vision, making it difficult to focus on the old woman. "She told me the truth, which is more than I received from *you*. I don't know why you weren't told, but—"

"She wasn't told because it changed nothing," said Hudson miserably. "For two hundred years we've been here, helping the curators, making sure the Doors are cared for, making sure the wayfarers who came through them seeking what they'd already lost were seen to and seen home in short order. Two hundred *years*. Ten generations of magpies have lived and died and seen *hundreds* of curators come through here, and when Elodina demanded her promise from Eider, we were exempt. She left us out of what she asked him. We were animals to her, inconsequential, even as we brought her everything she

needed, even though we had watched over the Doors for generations before she came, even though we'll be watching them
long after the last curator is gone. But he told Anya, and Anya
told Basia, and on, and on, and every one of them made the
same choices, made the same decisions, ran through the Doors
with the careless abandon of the first curator. But you know
what *did* change? What *did* become different?"

He hopped down from his perch, stalking toward the
counter's edge. Antsy couldn't take her eyes off of him. "They
were guilty. They felt like they were being punished. They
used the Doors anyway, but because they understood the consequences, they suffered for what they did. And they stayed,
and they traveled, and they suffered, because they knew."

"They needed to know because a choice you make without
knowing the consequences isn't any choice at all!" snapped
Antsy. "If they still used the doors, that was *their* decision. I
didn't know they were costing me anything."

"You thought all this was free?" Hudson spread his wings,
indicating the whole shop around them. "You should have
known better. Nothing is free, no matter what world you're in,
or what world you're from. Everywhere you've gone, you've paid
for what you received."

"But I . . ." Antsy stopped. The shop had taken care of her
from the moment she arrived, hadn't it? She'd always had a
place to sleep and a belly full of food, and she'd never been
sick, not even with a headache. The only times she'd needed
to stay in bed, she'd been too tired from using the doors to get
up, and on those days, soup and toast had been delivered to
her room by unseen hands. The Shop Where the Lost Things
Go took care of its contents, whatever their nature.

"I worked," she said, finally. "From the day I got here, I
worked, and I never had a salary from you. I never got a *penny*

for everything I did. And you were stealing from me. You were stealing my time—and you might be right, I might have given it freely, the same way Elodina did after she realized what was happening every time she used a door. We'll never know now."

"You received barter for what you did."

"That's true. But we are *damn* well going to tell whoever comes here next what it costs to use the doors, and we are never going to let it be forgotten again."

In the silence that stretched out after her proclamation, you could have heard ice melt. Finally, sounding dubious, Vineta asked, "You're staying?"

"Of course I'm staying," said Antsy. "Where would I go? If a door back to my original world opened, I couldn't go home. My mother is expecting a *child,* not . . . not this." She waved her hands, indicating the curve of her breast, the slope of her hip, and glared. "I may have been paid by your standards, but I've also been stolen from. I'm going to make damn sure we never do this to another child. It's not right, and it's not fair, and it's not going to happen anymore."

"The day's . . . the day's shopping . . ." began Vineta, and stopped as Antsy glared at her.

"No," she said. "Not today. Maybe not tomorrow, either. I'm willing to pay the toll, but not the way I have been; I'm not giving up weeks every day because you want perfect peaches or more shiny stickers for your calendar. You will be patient. You will be the adults you should have been all along. We'll go through the yard, we'll sort the things already here, and we'll travel when we don't have any other options. Do you understand me?"

"But—"

"No buts. Unless you want to open the doors yourself.

You told me you were fifteen when you came here. How long ago was that? Twenty years?" When Vineta cut her eyes away, Antsy scowled. "Less than twenty years to spend an entire lifetime, and you'd have let me do the same before you told me what it cost. You people don't deserve this place."

"Perhaps not, child, but we have it all the same." Vineta looked at her imperiously. "Go to your room."

Antsy barked a bitter laugh. "I'm not a little girl anymore, because of *you*. You don't get to tell me what to do."

"Fine, then, stay with us and start the morning's shopping," said Vineta. "You know you can't resist forever. The Doors will call you."

"Promise me," snapped Antsy. "Promise me you'll tell them if I can't. *Promise!*"

"Fine," said Vineta. "I promise."

Antsy shifted her attention to Hudson. "You should be ashamed," she told him. "Your people should always have kept the promise Eider made. Now you make it too."

"But the work . . ." he said, weakly.

Antsy stomped her foot.

"I promise!" he squawked.

"Good." Antsy, who was still a child in all the ways that counted, narrowed her eyes before she whirled on her heel and stormed up the stairs, leaving the pair behind her. Hudson looked at Vineta, ruffling his feathers.

"Surely she won't just disappear," he said. "The shop's aware, but not that delicate. Surely she'll be down for lunch."

"Surely?" asked Vineta. "When she's not even sure she wants to be here?" She leaned on her cane, glaring at the space where Antsy had been. Truly, youth was wasted on the young. "If the shop sees fit to be rid of her, it's doing us a favor. Promises are only binding if we agree to keep them."

Hudson cocked his head, looking uncomfortable, but said nothing.

When Antsy reached the top of the stairs, she stormed for the room that had always belonged to her, the room where she had been safe for so many nights. The room that had never hurt her.

The door was closed. She barely noticed, grabbing the knob and shoving inward, and she never saw the words written on the frame above her head. The door opened and she saw her room, and she stepped through and was on the sidewalk outside a closed thrift store, the sound of honking horns in the distance, the smell of car exhaust in the air. The sun was high in the afternoon sky, and everything was normal.

Antsy froze for a terrible moment before she whirled and tried to yank the door that had never been a Door before open again. It was locked. Slowly, she sank to the ground, pulling her knees against her chest, and sobbed.

12 NOT EVERYTHING CAN BE FOUND

ANTSY HUDDLED AND CRIED for so long that the cold of the concrete seeped through her thin cotton trousers. When she started to shiver, she finally stopped sobbing and pushed herself to her feet. That Door would have cost her, what, two days at most if the math was always the same. Two days was nothing compared to what she'd already lost. Two days didn't matter in the slightest. She was still the same person she'd been when she woke up that morning, and she could carry on with this.

She could. She could. She was going to have to.

She stood, and the feeling of static that sometimes meant she needed to find something specific in the shop filled her head. Turning a slow circle, she found the direction it was coming from and began to walk, taking inventory as she went.

She had nothing with her but the clothes she had been wearing and the note from Elodina, shoved down in her pocket and utterly without purpose here. At least she was wearing shoes. One instance where a careless footfall had driven a nail halfway through her heel had broken her of the habit of going barefoot. Face going blank, Antsy followed the sound of static, not fully aware that she was retracing her own footsteps from two years previous.

She wandered to the end of the block and turned, letting her feet choose the way. Suddenly, the static stopped, and so did she, in front of a house she had barely lived in long enough to recognize it. She didn't recognize the car in the driveway, either, a blue sedan that looked as incomprehensible as anything after so long without cars.

The front door opened. A woman emerged.

She was shorter than Antsy by several inches, which was horrifying to realize, with straight brown hair that brushed her shoulders. She started for her car, and then froze, one hand coming up to cover her mouth as she stared at Antsy.

Hope burst in Antsy's throat. Maybe her mother knew her. Maybe there was a similar static in her mother's head, and they were connected, because they were always meant to be together. Maybe. Cautiously, she raised one hand in a small wave, and the woman came toward her, and the hope grew even bigger.

"I'm sorry to stare," said her mother, polite as if she'd been speaking to any stranger. "It's just that your hair . . . my daughter had that kind of hair. Same color, same curl, everything."

"Oh," said Antsy, hope withering in an instant. She had dreamt of this day, of finding her mother again, without Tyler, a world where it was somehow just the two of them again. She hadn't had a baby sister long enough to be attached to the idea of her, and even though she knew it was selfish, those dreams had never included Abigail. Just Antsy and her mother, alone and happy and free.

They had never included her mother looking tired and worn and beaten down, and so sad, sad all the way down to her bones, with no idea who Antsy was. It was . . . hard. It was like looking through a window that could never be opened, and in that moment, Antsy felt like her heart caught halfway up with her body, aging in a great, traumatic jerk forward.

"It's not dyed," she said, desperate to continue the conversation somehow.

"No, it couldn't be. When you get that color out of a bottle, it always looks a little garish, even if it should be perfect. I used to try, when I was younger, and again for a while after my Antoinette . . ." Her mother stopped talking, voice tapering into silence, throat working as she swallowed. "I'm sorry. I'm being silly, and you don't know me at all. You just look so much like I always thought she would, if she got to be . . ." She sighed.

"I'm sorry you lost her," said Antsy. "Maybe you'll find her again someday." Maybe, in another fifteen years. She had the vague feeling that some people looked basically the same at twenty and at thirty; if she stayed out of the sun and took care of her skin, maybe she could pass herself off as her actual age when her birth certificate said twenty-five and her body said thirty-three.

Maybe not, but it was worth hoping for.

"That's all that keeps me going," said her mother, with a tight, dry laugh. "But it's not going to happen. There was a full police investigation. What they found was . . . on his computer, there were . . . pictures . . . My ex-husband is in prison for . . . for taking her away from me, and her little sister only knows her from pictures."

Abigail would grow up in a haunted house, surrounded by the ghost of a big sister who would never misbehave, never yell at her, never do anything wrong. It didn't seem fair . . . but it was better than growing up with a father who thought little girls were for hurting. They weren't. Abigail deserved to be protected. She deserved to be safe. She deserved to stay found.

Antsy smiled at her mother, who smiled back automatically, not understanding entirely why. "I'm sure she's a lovely little girl," she said. "I'm sorry for your loss, and I hope someday you find what you need to be happy."

"Thank you," said her mother, looking oddly brightened by the encounter.

The static was gone. As her mother walked to the car, Antsy found the strength to turn and walk away.

Whatever she'd been looking for, she had apparently managed to find it. She was halfway back to the shopping center—with no place better to go, it seemed like a reasonable point to return to—when the static came back, and she followed it down a smaller street and into the side yard of a house. There was no car in the driveway and the curtains were drawn, so she hoped it would be safe, and one teen girl didn't look like much of a robber. Still, she was tense and careful as she pushed her way past the shrubbery and stepped around the flowers, following the sound of static.

There, at the very back of the little strip of yard, huddled in the shadow of a rosemary plant, was a fluffy white kitten with darker markings on its paws and face and blood on its haunch. It whimpered when she picked it up. The static stopped for a moment, telling her she had found a lost thing, and then started again, more insistent, as the kitten burrowed against her chest, seeking comfort and shelter from the terrifying world that had done it such harm.

Antsy began walking again. The static was enough to guide her, and the weight of the kitten was comforting in her arms. So she kept going, tired as she was, confused and disoriented as she was, until the static led her up the walkway of a house she didn't know. She rang the bell, careful not to jostle the kitten in the process, and waited until she heard footsteps on the other side of the door, someone hurrying toward her. She managed not to shy away as the door opened and an older woman appeared.

"Can I help—" began the woman, before her eyes grew huge and she gasped, "Bootsie! Oh, where did you find her?"

She reached for the kitten, and Antsy shifted enough to make it easier, saying as she did, "Be careful, she's hurt. She was under some bushes, I heard her whimpering."

The woman took the kitten very gingerly out of Antsy's arms and looked her over, finally sighing. "She's an indoor cat," she said. "But I have to open the door when I go out, and she escaped. I've been looking for her for days. I promised a reward . . . If you want to come inside while I call my vet, I can get it for you."

"Oh, I didn't bring her back to you for a reward," said Antsy. "And I'm sure seeing the cat doctor will cost money. I'll be fine."

"No, really, I insist." The woman retreated into the house, kitten still clutched to her chest, and Antsy, who still had static buzzing through her head and had very little experience arguing with adults, followed after checking the doorframe carefully for writing. There was no resistance; sometimes a door is just a door. She did pause to close it behind her, in case the kitten found the energy to run again.

The woman was in the kitchen, a phone pressed to her ear, talking rapidly to someone. Antsy looked around with wide, wondering eyes, trying to remember what all these things were used for. The refrigerator was easy, as was the stove, but some of the shiny chrome and metal appliances were completely unfamiliar now, if they had ever been anything else.

The woman lowered her phone. "They can see us right away," she said. "I can't thank you enough. I'll get that reward money. Wait here."

Antsy nodded. The woman left the room. Antsy slowly drifted toward the fridge, which was covered in pieces of paper held up by bright, colorful magnets. Several were photographs, and her eyes fell on one in specific, showing two teenage girls, one with sleek brown hair and a crooked smile, the other so beautiful that her face was slightly blurred, as if even the camera hadn't been able to entirely focus on it. Antsy stared at the picture, the static getting louder in the back of her head, and knew that it was the next thing she needed to find.

The woman returned. Antsy indicated the picture. "Who's this?"

"My daughter, Angela, and her best friend, Seraphina. They go to the same special school." The woman offered her an envelope, and for a moment Antsy considered refusing to take it. She could probably find her own way if she had to. But it would be easier with money. Everything was easier with money, at least on the worlds that used it.

She took the envelope, not bothering to check the contents before she stuffed it into her pocket. Suddenly, she wondered whether she'd found the kitten because it was something lost that needed finding, or because it was the only reason to be here, in this kitchen, to see that picture, which clearly showed her the next thing she needed to find. Whether it was the girl or the place, she didn't know, but she supposed she'd find out soon.

"Thank you," she said gravely.

"No, thank *you* for bringing Bootsie home. Mommy was so worried about you, baby." That last was directed to the kitten, who huddled miserably in her arms.

She raised her head and focused on Antsy again. "I'm sorry to rush you out without at least offering something to drink, but I need to get Bootsie to the vet. Thank you again for bringing her back to me."

Antsy recognized a dismissal when she heard one. She nodded. "It was my pleasure."

The static grew stronger as she walked toward the door. She knew where she was going next. She just needed to get there.

13 BACK TO SCHOOL

WITH THE STATIC TO guide her, it wasn't hard for Antsy to find the bus station. She ran her finger down the list of destinations until one of them felt right, then traded half the contents of her envelope for a ticket and some change. The envelope went back into her pocket; the change went for a cheeseburger at the little kiosk inside the station, served hot and greasy and dripping with grilled onions and mustard. It tasted amazing. It tasted like coming home.

It sat in her stomach like a rock as she boarded the bus, one pretty teenager with no possessions, cramming herself into a window seat and leaning her forehead against the glass, trying to figure out how it could all have gone so wrong so quickly. She loved the shop, even after everything, and it needed her. She hadn't wanted to leave. Yes, it had stolen from her, but it was a place, and it wasn't the place's fault that the people who were supposed to take care of it had hidden things from her. She had to get back. She had to save the place she loved from Vineta, who Antsy was not convinced would keep her promise without someone to make her keep it, and all the other people like her, the ones who would allow children to spend themselves to make their own lives a little easier. And yes, some children would choose the doors anyway—the addiction of novelty was real—but they would do so understanding what it cost.

They would *understand*.

Someone settled in the seat next to her and tried to make conversation. She ignored them as the bus pulled out, watching the land roll by outside in silence. There was so much land. She'd always known worlds were big, but she had been seeing them in two- and three-hour installments for years. This was the longest she'd looked at anything outside the shop since the day she ran away. She didn't know how to focus on this much space anymore. It was so much.

She rode until the bus pulled up to a stop on a long green highway, miles from any town. The static grew louder. Antsy rose, walking to the front of the bus, and when the doors hissed open, she stepped down, stepped off, stepped out into that big world.

There was a building in the distance, like a manor house, tall and imposing and, as she walked toward it, increasingly ridiculous. It looked like it had been built the same way the shop was, one piece at a time, until the whole had no real harmony with itself. She kept walking, studying the mismatched curtains in the windows, the patches of contrasting paint. It looked familiar.

It looked like home.

There was a sign hanging from the eaves, the words coming clear as she finished walking up the long driveway to the porch. ELEANOR WEST'S HOME FOR WAYWARD CHILDREN, it read, in large letters. Below, in smaller letters, it continued, NO SOLICITATION, NO VISITORS, NO QUESTS.

Antsy swallowed. She was a visitor. Was she on a quest? Still, she walked to the door, raised her hand, and knocked. The static grew briefly louder, then burst like a popped soap bubble, replaced by silence.

Silence, and enough time to feel like she'd made a terrible mistake before she heard footsteps, and the door swung open to reveal a woman not that much younger than Vineta. Her hair was fine and white, standing out in a dandelion corona from her head, and her wrinkled face was kind. She was wearing more colors than Antsy knew could be worn at once, like she had looked at a rainbow once, and thought, "Oh, much too subtle."

Antsy blinked. So did the woman. Then, slowly, the woman began to smile. "The morning dew told me we might have a new student arriving today," she said. "Come on inside, dear, and we'll start getting you registered. And don't worry—the only writing above my door is what I put there. You're safe here at the school."

Hesitantly, Antsy returned her smile and stepped inside as the woman moved out of the way to let her pass.

This time, when the door closed, it didn't sound like an ending.

It sounded like the beginning of something new.